HUNGRY LIKE DE WOLFE

INSPIRED BY KATHRYN LE VEQUE'S WARWOLFE

DE WOLFE PACK
THE SERIES

ANNA MARKLAND

COVER ART BY STEVEN NOVAK

Text copyright by the Author.

This work was made possible by special permission through the de Wolfe Pack Connected World publishing program and WolfeBane Publishing, a dba of Dragonblade Publishing. All characters, scenes, events, plots and related elements appearing in the original World of de Wolfe Pack connected series by Kathryn Le Veque Novels, Inc. remains the exclusive copyrighted and/or trademarked property of Kathryn Le Veque Novels, Inc., or the affiliates or licensors.

All characters created by the author of this novel remain the copyrighted property of the author.

DE WOLFE PACK: THE SERIES

By Alexa Aston
Rise of de Wolfe

By Amanda Mariel
Love's Legacy

By Anna Markland
Hungry Like de Wolfe

By Autumn Sands
Reflection of Love

By Barbara Devlin
Lone Wolfe: Heirs of Titus De Wolfe Book 1
The Big Bad De Wolfe: Heirs of Titus De Wolfe Book 2
Tall, Dark & De Wolfe: Heirs of Titus De Wolfe Book 3

By Cathy MacRae
The Saint

By Christy English
Dragon Fire

By Hildie McQueen
The Duke's Fiery Bride

By Kathryn Le Veque
River's End

By Lana Williams
Trusting the Wolfe

By Laura Landon
A Voice on the Wind

By Leigh Lee
Of Dreams and Desire

By Mairi Norris
Brabanter's Rose

By Marlee Meyers
The Fall of the Black Wolf

By Mary Lancaster
Vienna Wolfe

By Meara Platt
Nobody's Angel
Bhrodi's Angel
Kiss an Angel

By Mia Pride
The Lone Wolf's Lass

By Ruth Kaufman
My Enemy, My Love

By Sarah Hegger
Bad Wolfe on the Rise

By Scarlett Cole
Together Again

By Victoria Vane
Breton Wolfe Book 1
Ivar the Red Book 2
The Bastard of Brittany Book 3

By Violetta Rand
Never Cry de Wolfe

For Family Tree Researchers Everywhere

Keep Digging

Two great medieval dynasties come together.
Le Veque's De Wolfe Pack and
Markland's Montbryce~FitzRam family.
The world will never be the same.

Table of Contents

Ms. Smith 1
First Meeting 9
Inheritance 20
It's a Date 28
Tapas for Two 34
Apologies 44
Guilt 48
Dinner for Two 59
Hungry Wolf 67
Madness 76
Explosive Information 83
Euston Station 89
Virginia Water 95
Who Knew? 102
The Penny Drops 112
A Token 116
A Goldmine 119
Goodbye 122
A Wedding 128
Honeymoon 135
Victory 140
Epilogue 145
About Anna 150
More Anna Markland 152

MS. SMITH

London, England 2006

ANNE PICKED UP the phone when line one buzzed. Twirling the curly black cord around one finger, she tucked the receiver under her chin. "Good morning. *Digging Up Your Roots.* How can I help?"

When there was no response, she pushed back in the state-of-the-art ergonomic office chair, slipped off her high heel shoes and put her feet up on the mahogany desk, ankles crossed. Sheer stockings caused her skirt to ride up her thighs, but there was no one to see the old-fashioned suspenders she loved, so she didn't bother fixing it. They were good-looking legs for a twenty-seven year old, if she did think so herself, and tights had never been her thing.

Wiggling her toes, she tapped the end of her Parker ballpoint on the pink message pad. "Hello? Anybody there?"

"I'd like to speak to the head of your research department."

The deep baritone voice raised goosebumps on her nape.

Dreamy.

However, the caller's failure to return the greeting, and the absence of the word *please*, quickly brought her back to reality. The fake-sounding *Oxford* accent was a dead giveaway. The man on the other end of the line was one of those snooty types who is certain he's descended from aristocracy.

She'd come across many of them in her profession. They invariably assumed people who answered the telephone were brainless minions.

However, they were her bread and butter, rich clients who paid large sums of money for proof of the blue blood in their veins. It always struck her as ironic that if they were in fact descended from nobility they were easier to trace. Reliable genealogical records for peasants and the working class were virtually non-existent prior to the 1700's.

She inhaled the subtle lavender lingering in the air from the diffuser, took her feet off the desk, slipped her shoes back on, sat up straight and pulled down her skirt. It was easier to feign a posh accent if you were sitting like a lady. "Whom may I say is calling?"

Another pause, then, "Blaise Emery Quentin de Wolfe, the Third."

She bit down on the knuckle of her index finger to stifle the urge to laugh out loud. She was speaking to yet another wealthy snob clinging to the *de* in his surname and probably anxious to prove his Norman ancestry. With renewed interest in Normandy after last year's 60th anniversary of D-Day, otherwise down-to-earth, sensible men were clamoring for acceptance into membership of the exclusive *Sons of the Conquest*.

She was extremely proud of her own Norman heritage, but it was beyond her comprehension why anyone would want to be associated with a bunch of elitist chauvinists. The SOC insisted on remaining a male-only club, despite attempts by many, including herself, to get the rules changed. They also restricted their ranks to those who could prove their conquering ancestors were men of *pure* Norman lineage, apparently unaware the Conqueror himself was a bastard.

She perched her reading glasses on the end of her nose and crossed her legs. "Anne Smith speaking, Mr. de Wolfe. Am I to understand you wish to commission a research project?"

That never failed to throw them off balance. There was no more common, unaristocratic English surname than Smith; *Anne* was a one-syllable Christian name beginning with a vowel that most people had forgotten within two minutes of being introduced to her.

"Smith?"

She chewed her bottom lip. "*Anne* Smith," she reiterated. "What is it you want to research, Mr. de Wolfe?"

He cleared his throat. Satisfaction rippled that she seemed to have rendered him speechless.

"I'd like you to confirm my ancestral roots. Shouldn't be a problem. I'm a descendant of Gaetan de Wolfe, a Norman knight who fought at the Battle of Hastings. There's extensive research available, carried out by my great grandfather, but I need to have it verified."

Ka-ching! Was that the sound of a cash register?

※

BLAISE HANDED THE cordless phone back to his butler, rested his head on the back of the threadbare Georgian sofa and peered up at the mural painted on the parlor ceiling generations before by Ford Madox Brown.

"Problem, sir?" Michael asked.

He might have known his long time servant would detect his unease. "We'll have to get the Brown restored soon."

He made the same observation every time he looked up at the faded and cracked mural, but they both knew there was no money in the dwindling De Wolfe Hall coffers for the project.

Michael smiled indulgently. "Any luck with the contact you were given, sir?"

Blaise wrinkled his nose and shifted his weight, making a mental note to add the job of getting the uncomfortable sofa cleaned and resprung to the long list. "I'm not sure. I have an appointment for tomorrow morning, but the woman didn't come across as very professional. She answers her own phone."

Michael coughed politely. "She came highly recommended."

It was true the *Sons of the Conquest* had advised him to seek the documentation he needed from *Digging Up Your Roots*. Once he got to the office, he'd make a list of other possible professionals, fearing from the too-cute name it wasn't a well-run business. Maybe she'd worked out a kickback deal with the *Sons*. "Being obliged to provide proof from a professional genealogist is absurd," he complained. "Why can't they simply accept my great grandfather's research?"

Michael looked up at the mural. "As you've said, sir."

"Her name is Smith, for heaven's sake, and she'll probably charge an arm and a leg. It's an expense I can't afford."

He checked his watch, then heaved himself off the sofa. "Best get a move on. I'm already going to be late to the city, and if I miss the next train…"

"Yes, sir," Michael replied, making no remark about the lack of enthusiasm Blaise found increasingly difficult to conceal. He was a good barrister with many triumphs in difficult cases to his credit. He'd always loved his chosen profession, but his cantankerous boss's failure to grant him a well-deserved full partnership rankled.

The other matter that remained unspoken between him and his servant was a reality they were both aware of. If he wasn't accepted into the *Sons of the Conquest*, he stood to lose De Wolfe Hall.

Just after five o'clock, Anne shut down the computers and unplugged the aromatherapy diffuser after inhaling a last deep breath of the lavender. She made her way to the kitchen where the appetizing aroma of short ribs simmering in the slow cooker provided a different kind of satisfaction and made her stomach growl.

She zapped a packet of frozen steamed sweet peas for three minutes in the microwave then plated up the ribs, eased open the perforation of the pea packet, poured a generous glass of Malbec and *voilà*, a meal fit for…

One.

She perched on a high-backed stool at the breakfast counter to eat. It never felt as lonely as sitting by herself at the kitchen table.

The formal dining room had also been out of the question since Geoff's death. It held too many memories of elegant dinner parties, laughter, stimulating conversation, cleaning up together afterwards, and then—off to bed.

She sniffed back tears as she finished the last of the solitary meal. She hadn't cried since the first year when she'd almost gone mad with grief—and anger. Captain

Geoffrey Smith had volunteered for a second tour in Iraq. What was left of him had come home in a wooden box.

FIRST MEETING

THE FOLLOWING MORNING Blaise took an early train into the city and eventually managed to get a cab outside Waterloo Station. He gave the driver the address and sank back in the seat, trying not to go over every detail of the frustrating telephone conversation he'd had shortly after dawn with some fellow calling from China. If they were going to harangue him about selling De Wolfe Hall could they not at least pay attention to time zones? With every word echoing on the long distance line, it was like trying to communicate with an alien on the moon.

He'd not slept well and was still filled with misgivings about *Digging Up Your Roots*. The previous day at work he'd compiled a list of alternatives from a Google search and intended to spend his lunch hour making appointments if Ms. Smith didn't come up to snuff. She was probably an elderly spinster with a bun, although he had to admit her sultry voice was pleasant, even alluring. But then people often sounded different on the phone.

The taxi pulled up outside a well-kept Georgian mansion, one of a stunning row of identical, blindingly white four-story homes on St. George's Terrace, not far from Victoria Station.

He rolled down the window and peered up at the impressive structure. "Are you sure this is it?"

The cockney scowled. "It's the address you gave me, *guv*."

Not convinced, he nevertheless hefted the briefcase with his great grandfather's tome of research, climbed out and paid the fare. The small tip he included earned him another scowl before the taxi sped off.

The polished brass plate affixed to one of the portico columns bore the inscription *Digging Up Your Roots, Professional Genealogical Services.*

Still doubtful, he took the four or five steps to the black lacquered door, rang the bell and straightened his tie.

He turned back to the busy street and noticed the steps had been newly scrubbed, the edges pumiced white. That level of pride in appearance was rare in London these days. How did Smith afford the rent for such a place?

The security buzzer took him by surprise. Tightening his grip on the handle of the briefcase he turned the brass knob and opened the door.

The tiled hallway was nondescript, clean but devoid of decoration, almost spartan. An expensive-looking red bicycle leaned against the curved wall, a sturdy helmet hanging from its handlebars. He shook his head at the foolhardiness of anyone who rode a bike in London's horrendous traffic.

He looked about, unsure where to go. There was a white door to the left of a spiral staircase, but the small brass plaque engraved with the word PRIVATE excluded that possibility.

"Up here."

He put a foot on the bottom stair and looked up. Struck by a sudden wave of panic, he gripped the banister with his free hand, not sure if it was the effect of four floors of white staircase spindles making him dizzy or the unexpectedly beautiful face bestowing a stunning smile. Blonde curls flowed over the top railing like Rapunzel's fairytale tresses.

Ms. Smith obviously wasn't a bespectacled elderly spinster with a bun.

He began the ascent feeling as though he was climbing to the gallery in some out of the way intimate theatre.

Her pleasing voice drifted down to him like a siren call. "I know it's silly. I like having my office on the fourth floor. The room is the right size and I'm away from the traffic, which is important when you're researching."

Panting, he reached the top landing, feeling much older than his thirty-one years. He ought to get back to the fitness level he'd worked hard to achieve at Uni. His days as captain of the Oxford rowing eight seemed long ago and far away.

She eyed him as he paused for breath. "You need to exercise more," she said, extending her hand.

He was tempted to make a retort, but the twinkle in her wide eyes spoke of teasing rather than censure, so he let it go. If she noticed his palm was sweaty as she gripped his hand in a firm handshake she didn't give any sign of it.

Anne Smith was definitely not what he'd expected. Her poise, charm and beauty filled his spinning head with errant thoughts of asking her on a date. But then the weight he'd hauled up in the briefcase reminded him of the reason for his mission.

She pointed to his burden. "Looks impressive. My office is this way."

He made the mistake of glancing over the railing before following her. The vortex of the stairway sucked him in. The fear of heights he thought he'd overcome long ago took hold as vertigo blurred his vision. Sweat broke out on his brow. His knees trembled.

She took his hand and led him to safety. The reassuring touch of her warm skin was a relief but the loss of control was embarrassing.

"I have the same problem," she said. "That's why I prefer to live on the first floor."

He loosened his tie as the turmoil in his belly subsided. "You live here?"

"Yes. An ancestor built this house for his wife. It's been in the family ever since."

※

Take that tidbit of information and stuff it in your expensive Burberry briefcase, Anne thought as the pompous man staggered into her office.

"The lavender will help you regain your equilibrium," she said.

He sniffed the air suspiciously. "I wondered what that smell was."

Trust a man to refer to the soothing scent of lavender as a *smell*. She'd bet he was mortified at the weakness he'd shown. Stiff upper lip and all that. She'd also lay odds the great grandfather whose research he'd promised to bring was a very *proper* British army officer, probably served in India.

She had to admit, however, that Blaise *Whatever Whatever* de Wolfe the Third, wasn't what she'd expected. His voice was huskier and deeper than on the phone, though there'd been a hint of disbelieving falsetto in his question about her actually living in the house. The color had rushed back into his ashen face upon learning she owned the mansion.

His well-muscled frame suggested he'd once been a jock. He'd let himself go a bit but was still an attractive man—tall, lots of thick, glossy black hair. Good complexion, slightly tanned. The grey English-style Savile Row suit added to his distinguished look and she recognised the striped tie of Magdalen College. She'd been right about the Oxford background.

Realizing she was staring, she ushered him to sit in one of the two leather armchairs in front of the hearth.

"Feeling better?"

He nodded, still clutching the briefcase he'd brought.

The July heat ruled out a fire, and she rarely lit one now she had central heating. Roaring fires were for cuddling up with someone you loved, and there'd been no one since...

Re-focussing on the tasteful lacquered screen that concealed the grate—a treasured souvenir from China—she sat facing him in the other armchair and crossed her legs, confident in their power to draw the male eye. If they didn't do it, the shiny black three-inch heels usually did.

She was disappointed when he settled the briefcase at his feet and scanned his surroundings. "This is a splendid office," he said.

Probably expected a dingy hole in a Bayswater basement.

She was smugly aware of the room's ability to inspire confidence in potential clients. Large windows, tastefully draped and swagged, quality leather furniture, the mahogany desk tucked discreetly in one corner, two oversized computer screens, the ergonomic chair, and the *pièce de résistance*—walls lined with bookshelves laden with tome after tome of leather-bound genealogical reference books.

They were impressive, but she rarely cracked them open. The main reason for the diffuser, apart from the fact she loved lavender, was to mask the distinctive odor of old book-bindings.

Most of her research was done online or in libraries, public records offices and sometimes in the dwindling number of stately mansions. She even took the occasional trip if necessary to delve into the enormous repository of Mormon records in Salt Lake City.

"Tell me what you need, Mr. de Wolfe," she said, pulling the hem of her skirt closer to her knees in an effort to draw his eye.

It worked. He stared at her legs as, with one capable hand, he heaved a nine-inch-thick wad of yellowed papers from the bag and thrust them at her. "It's simply a question of signing off on these in support of my membership application for the *Sons of the Conquest*. They recommended you."

Otherwise you'd have run a mile in the opposite direction!

Most people would wrinkle their noses at the musty odor, but to Anne the documents represented a mine of information where she might strike gold. She accepted the weighty pile with both hands, almost salivating at the prospect of untying the faded and frayed red ribbon that held the sheaf together. How long had it been since anyone delved into the treasures within the pages?

However, she was obliged to offer the usual professional word of caution. "We must bear in mind that this research was done three generations ago. Records then weren't as verifiable as they are now, with the Internet, and so on."

She lost her train of thought when she realized she was gazing into the most unusual turquoise colored eyes she had ever seen.

"But my great grandfather was apparently a very meticulous man," he protested with a frown.

As she might have expected, he'd shot down her first piece of cautionary advice. "Well, we'll see what we can find. How far back did he manage to get?"

"To the Vikings," he replied without hesitation.

She had a suspicion then she might as well toss the pile into the waste bin. "I see."

Blaise closed the front door of *Digging Up Your Roots* hoping he'd done the right thing in leaving his family's research in Anne Smith's hands.

The interview had left him confused. On the one hand she seemed anxious to make a start on the project, but then she'd voiced all kinds of reservations. She'd been particularly skeptical about any verifiable link with Vikings.

Surely she wasn't the bike rider?

He supposed he'd been thrown off balance by her unexpected sophisticated confidence—and those legs!

Of all the inconvenient times to have an attack of vertigo. The lavender had helped though.

A final glance back at the impressive house confirmed his suspicion she must have access to private money. It was puzzling.

The briefcase felt a lot lighter so he decided to walk to his offices near the Supreme Court. He'd let himself go and it was time to get back in shape. Once the problem of De Wolfe Hall was solved, he'd look into renewing his gym membership. Or perhaps purchase a bike.

As he waited to cross at the traffic signals on Vauxhall Bridge Road, it occurred to him his worry over the Viking connection was unfounded. The important thing was confirmation of the purity of Gaetan de Wolfe's bloodline. He had to trust Anne Smith was astute enough to find the proof of it.

Inheritance

Anne spent the remainder of the day printing off pedigree reports and tying up loose ends on a number of commissions already underway. The thick stack of yellowed paper sitting on the corner of her desk beckoned enticingly. She couldn't wait to untie the ribbon and get started on it.

Research nowadays certainly wasn't always easy, and she disliked the tedious data entry part of her profession. However, technology had brought enormous advances. The software database was an invaluable tool, one of many that de Wolfe's ancestor didn't have at his disposal. His work held the promise of interesting reading and a journey into the past—family trees drawn painstakingly by hand; personal anecdotes lamentably missing from many modern ancestral histories.

Every time she glanced at the dog-eared pile, she tried to conjure an image of the man who had compiled it, but the only face that floated into her mind's eye was Blaise de Wolfe's.

She wondered if her client had inherited his intriguing turquoise eyes and dark hair from his great grandfather. On first learning of his commission she'd been ready to treat him with disdain, and yet there was something attractive about him. He didn't seem the type to be anxious to join an organisation like the *Sons of the Conquest*.

She decided to take his material downstairs to read in the parlor after dinner. Once again seated at the counter to eat her slow-baked chicken, she glanced at the red gingham cloth covering the kitchen table, shrugging away a bizarre notion to invite Blaise de Wolfe to sit there when he came to discuss her findings.

Resolved not to dwell on the past—at least not her own past—she drank the rest of her wine, poured another glass, and decided to leave the dishes for the morning.

Tongue clamped firmly between her teeth, she held her breath and pulled the frayed ribbon loose. The treasure chest had been unlocked for the first time in who knew how long.

But she hesitated. It might turn out to be Pandora's Box.

Laughing away the notion as foolish, she took the top first dozen or so pages into the parlor, filled with a sense of anticipation she hadn't felt in along while.

※

BLAISE DE WOLFE the Second had always insisted every meal be served in the formal dining room, which at one time had been the Great Hall of the house built in the reign of Elizabeth the First. In his view, only servants ate at kitchen tables.

Even after his mother died and there was just the two of them, Blaise and his father dined at the solid oak table which sat in splendid isolation in the centre of the cavernous room.

Somehow he couldn't bring himself to break the habit though it was ludicrous that he sat alone at the head of a table that accommodated twelve, without the extension added.

The stone floor kept the high-ceilinged room cold even now at the height of summer. Yet he couldn't recall the last time a fire had blazed in the huge fireplace. Something to do with the flue or the damper, he'd forgotten which. Perhaps a fire would get rid of the smell of damp.

Or a diffuser like the one in Anne Smith's office.

It wasn't surprising the place smelled old. Thomas de Wolfe had built the house after purchasing and demolishing an old manor that had belonged to Westminster Abbey since before the Norman Conquest. The Elizabethan carpenters employed to work on the interior had carved an enormous oak screen which took up one whole wall of the dining room, its Corinthian pilasters and archway done in the style of the Italian Renaissance. It was a masterpiece.

A later, evidently less enlightened de Wolfe, had smothered the wood with dark brown paint, most of which was now peeling off. Restored and refurbished, the screen would resurrect the room, but again there was no money for such grand projects.

How expensive could a diffuser be?

He picked at the chicken cacciatore Michael had served, bothered by the constantly recurring notion of how ridiculous it was that servants still cooked and served his food. It was a lifestyle his family had clung to, though they should have abandoned it in his grandfather's day.

The crumbling country mansion, as well as his father's gambling addiction and fondness for alcohol, had already drained the family fortune, and Blaise spent nearly all his earnings as a successful barrister on exorbitant electricity and other monthly bills.

Deer roamed the parkland, swans nested and herons waded in the lake, but the ancient tenant cottages had fallen into disrepair and maintaining the two hundred unproductive acres drained cash. And the land taxes! Riding through the estate had been one of Blaise's greatest pleasures growing up. But the Arabians were long gone.

If things got much worse, he'd be forced to buy a bike and cycle to the train station. It might help get some of the weight off. He wouldn't have the first idea about what kind of bike to get, but supposed he could ask Anne Smith. Maybe that's how she kept in such good shape.

He shoved aside the half-eaten meal, mildly irritated that he seemed preoccupied with the woman.

His faithful butler's footsteps echoed on the stone floor. Michael offered the bottle of Malbec. "More wine, sir?"

He didn't have the heart to let the few remaining

servants go but couldn't afford to offer them a pension. He'd often invited the old man to call him by his given name—to no avail. "Thank you," he replied, though he'd already consumed two glasses. "Then I'll be fine. You can have the rest of the night to yourself."

Michael poured the wine, wiped off the neck of the bottle with a napkin and set it back on its silver-plated tray. "Any luck with Ms. Smith this morning?"

Blaise eyed a tiny fruit fly drowning in his wine, but didn't point it out to Michael, who obviously hadn't noticed, a sure sign the man's legendary attention to detail was failing. "She accepted the commission."

"Best of luck with it then, sir. Goodnight."

As soon as the butler had left he fished the corpse out of his wine and flicked it away. His thoughts drifted once more to the surprising blonde he'd met at the interview. "Wonder what Ms. Smith is doing for fun?" he said aloud. "I doubt she's playing with drowned flies."

Fists clenched, he looked around the dining room. Dated wallpaper had faded and was peeling in places. Family portraits badly needed restoration, the oils cracked so badly on some it was impossible to make out the sitter's face. The Victorian sideboard, huge table and rickety chairs could pass for what was popularly called *distressed* these days.

Cobwebs festooned the wrought-iron light fixtures that hung on long, black chains from the ceiling. Most of the bulbs were missing. During the day, light flooded in from the floor-to-ceiling mullioned windows. At night the place was reminiscent of a dungeon.

If he shouted out his frustrations, the walls would just echo them back.

Based on the quality of furnishings in her office he'd guess Anne Smith's home would put his to shame.

What kind of world was it where a Smith prospered and a de Wolfe was being sucked under by a mountain of debt?

He gulped his wine, regretting the selfish thought. His predicament was hardly Anne Smith's fault. She was an attractive, successful woman whose forbears had obviously done a better job of managing their assets.

The barely concealed excitement in her green eyes when he handed her his great grandfather's research had driven away his doubts about her—and sparked the interest of his cock, something no woman had achieved since Tessa's betrayal.

Why would a single woman live in such a big house? She was probably happily married. That was strangely depressing.

He drained the wine and contemplated simply polishing off the bottle.

IT'S A DATE

AN INSISTENT RINGING jolted Anne awake. Disoriented, she tried unsuccessfully to prevent the de Wolfe papers from sliding off her lap as she struggled to sit up in the deep leather armchair.

Reaching for the cordless phone on the occasional table, she blinked twice at the mantle clock. "Who calls at close to midnight?" she muttered aloud.

Her throat tightened. The last time she'd received a call late at night…

"Hello?" she croaked, rubbing one eye.

"Er…Blaise de Wolfe here. I didn't wake you, did I?"

His deep voice soothed her frazzled nerves, despite her surprise. "No," she lied. "But it is late."

"Yes, sorry about that. Have you had a chance to look at my pedigree?"

He thinks I have nothing else to do.

However, she had quoted him a steep fee for her

services, so perhaps he was entitled. She stared guiltily at the papers scattered at her feet, reluctant to admit she'd intended to glance at them but ended up reading almost half. "A few pages, the preamble," she lied again.

"Good, good. Can we meet for coffee tomorrow to discuss it? Or lunch perhaps, if that's more convenient."

Whoa!

"I haven't read enough to formulate a professional opinion yet."

The lies had to stop!

There was a long pause. "It would be a chance to get to know each other better."

She took off her reading glasses and pinched the bridge of her nose. She couldn't deny she'd found him attractive, in a pompous sort of way, but then there was Geoff. Or rather the ghost of Geoff. "You mean a date?"

"We got along well yesterday."

His take on the meeting was interesting. Her instinct was to refuse. Mixing business with pleasure was never a good idea.

That was just plain ridiculous. Since Geoff's death

her life had been nothing but business. *Pleasure* with another man was a daunting prospect, even if it was only a lunch.

An unexpected urge to stretch like a cat took hold. His suggestion of a date had thrown her off balance, but it was exciting to think she'd drawn the eye of a rich, attractive man. Dredging up her courage, she asked, "What did you have in mind?"

She rolled her eyes. Dozing off after too much wine had made her throat dry and the flippant question probably sounded like she was the queen of the dating scene.

"You know your area best. What do you suggest?"

She had no idea, since she hadn't ventured out to eat alone in a restaurant in three years, but her gaze fell on a glossy local magazine she'd left on the table after perusing it the day before. "Tazzi's on Gillinghall Street is good. Tapas. Venetian."

She could picture him frowning.

"Hmm. I've had Spanish tapas but not Venetian. Sounds good. I'll look forward to it. Shall I meet you there? 12:15? Do I need to make a reservation?"

She hurriedly scanned the article but could find no mention of reservations. "Er…perhaps. It's a date," she replied.

She clutched the phone to her breast, then hurriedly checked to make sure she'd pressed the END button. If he hadn't rung off he'd surely be able to hear the loud beating of her heart.

※

HAVING HEMMED AND hawed for hours about calling Anne Smith, Blaise hadn't realized how late it was. Not surprising she sounded half asleep, although he'd noticed the same sultry edge to her voice during the interview.

She probably thought he was annoyingly weird, phoning in the middle of the night. It was unreasonable to expect she'd read all the research. She likely had several other contracts, although he was paying an exorbitant fee which she'd quoted without batting an eye.

Focussed on her long, silky legs, he'd agreed without hesitation.

He could confidently and effectively argue a point of law in front of the Supreme Court, but the fickle Tessa had knocked his instincts about women for six. He'd trusted that she loved him, but...

Determined not to descend into the bottomless pit of second-guessing the past, he put his feet up on the worn sofa and tried unsuccessfully to get comfortable.

Anne Smith might also turn out to be a gold digger, although her lifestyle didn't suggest a lack of funds, and in her line of work she must have come across eligible wealthy men.

Maybe she was divorced. He should have paid attention. Was she wearing a wedding ring?

He was attracted to her, he couldn't deny it, but what did he have to offer a woman? A decrepit, old, not-so-stately mansion, a mountain of debt and an empty bank account—the principal reasons that proving the purity of his Norman lineage was vital.

His apprehension about dating was pathetic. He folded his arms and eyed the empty wine bottle with disgust. It had taken a skinful of Malbec to bolster his courage, but that wasn't surprising considering he hadn't trusted his heart to anyone since his fiancée's betrayal.

⟫⟫⟪⟪

ANNE PRESSED REDIAL twice then hit the END button each time before the dial-tone began. A date with

Blaise de Wolfe was really out of the question. Very unprofessional. If she hadn't been so tired, she'd never have agreed. He'd caught her off guard and the wine had muddled her thinking.

The phone bounced off the couch when she threw it down in frustration.

What was wrong with accepting a harmless lunch date with an attractive, well-educated man? A successful barrister.

Geoff was dead. She wasn't. Why did he still have such a strong hold on her?

TAPAS FOR TWO

B LAISE SPENT THE morning in his office going over several important case files, but couldn't concentrate, his thoughts on lunch with Anne Smith. He had a vague idea where Gillinghall Street was, but searched Google maps to make sure. It turned out to be only about a mile from his offices near the Supreme Court in Parliament Square, so he decided to walk instead of taking a cab. It was time to get some weight off and Pimlico was a pleasant district, not far from Buckingham Palace.

His plan was to arrive early so he'd have a chance to peruse the menu, but Anne was already seated. The place was crowded, but she stood out like a welcoming beacon. The white top with a crisp-looking pale green overblouse suited her. He was mildly disappointed he couldn't see her shapely legs.

He felt strangely dizzy when she greeted him with a nervous smile. Perhaps he'd overdone the walking exercise.

The waiter wheeled out the white leather chair that would look more at home in an office, flicked the napkin open with a snap and laid it across his lap.

It gave him a momentary opportunity to sneak a peek under the table-for-two, pleased to see she wore a skirt, not pants.

"Thanks for taking time to meet me," he said, glad he'd made the decision to ask her out.

She gripped the laminated menu. "No problem. It's not far from my office."

Her uneasiness puzzled him. Maybe she *was* married, though she didn't strike him as a woman who would agree to a *date* if she was.

He scanned the decor. "Interesting mix of styles, industrial and elegant."

She nodded. "Lots of windows."

"Something smells delicious," he remarked.

She nodded.

He steepled his hands, tapped his fingers together and glanced at the menu. "So what do you recommend?"

She flattened her palms on the white tablecloth and stared at the choices. He fixed his gaze on the bright red nail polish and long, elegant fingers, dismayed to see a wedding ring. But it was on the wrong hand.

He looked up, disconcerted to discover she was staring at him. "Sorry. I was admiring your ring," he said lamely, mesmerized by her green eyes.

She clenched her fist and thumbed the gold band. "Don't worry. I'm not married."

He reached for her hand. "You wouldn't have come if you were."

There was a momentary glint of gratitude in her eyes, but she withdrew her hand quickly. "I can't recommend anything because I've never been here before."

This partially explained her nervousness, but why had she led him to believe she frequented the place?

"I read about it in a magazine," she admitted. "I don't eat out much."

The hint of regret in her voice gave him pause. Outwardly she seemed like a woman of the world, a sophisticate, but he sensed it was a veneer that hid a sadness. Someone had hurt her. He knew what that was all about.

The waiter hovered. "Anything to drink?"

"I'll have a glass of the Pinot Grigio," she replied.

"San Pellegrino sparkling water for me."

She frowned.

"Important meeting at the office this afternoon," he explained. "Otherwise I'd have the Malbec."

Her first relaxed smile poured fuel on the interest already simmering in his balls.

"Malbec is my favorite wine, but I thought I'd have white. I've some serious research to do later."

That reminder trimmed his sails. He checked the bill of fare, resenting having to make a mental calculation of what the meal was going to cost. He had the universally accepted Luncheon Vouchers in his wallet, but this wasn't company business. "Made any progress?" he asked, trying to sound nonchalant.

The waiter reappeared with the beverages, poured the carafe of wine into a wineglass and the sparkling water into a tumbler. "Are you ready to order?"

Anne raised her eyebrows, reflecting his opinion of the waiter's lack of cordiality. "I'll have the asparagus salad with quail eggs and black truffles."

"And the pizzetta with tomatoes and roasted peppers for me," he said, opting for the cheapest item available, though the prices were reasonable considering this was Pimlico.

"Normally customers take two items," the unsmiling waiter said patronizingly, scribbling down their order. "They are small servings. Tapas, *capisci*?"

Anne shook her head. "I'm planning to leave room for the pistachio tiramisu," she replied.

Blaise experienced a sudden irrational desire to spare no expense in an effort to impress this woman. It compounded his resentment at his financial predicament.

The waiter lifted his chin, retrieved the menus and departed.

"Not the friendliest," she said with a grin, raising her glass.

"I'll say, and the Italian accent is definitely fake." He clinked his glass against hers. "Here's to a productive relationship, Anne Smith."

He was disappointed when she looked away and sipped the Pinot without acknowledging his toast.

※

CONFLICTING EMOTIONS SWIRLED in Anne's heart. Simply being here with another man was disloyal to Geoff.

She clenched her fists in her lap. That was another

ridiculous notion. Her husband had volunteered to go to Iraq against her wishes.

She was more attracted to Blaise de Wolfe than she wanted to be. His grey summer blazer, stylish yet classic at the same time, had drawn the appreciative eye of many of the female diners. Summer slacks emphasized his long legs. The college tie should have looked absurd, yet he carried off the combination of casual and formal seemingly without effort. He was easily the most handsome man in the busy restaurant. Finding him attractive felt wrong but right at the same time. It was perplexing.

She'd ordered white wine and asparagus, both of which she disliked, then stated her intention to follow with dessert, something she rarely did, especially at lunchtime.

Her brain had evidently closed down. Yet the man seated across from her was touching off exciting physical sensations she hadn't felt in years.

She knew from a quick perusal of Google that he was a successful barrister. Numerous high profile cases were cited. She imagined how dignified he'd look in wig and gown, his deep voice uttering *M'Lud* with great solemnity. "Do you work in the City, Mr. de

Wolfe?" she asked in a voice that came out alarmingly hoarse.

"Please, it's Blaise. I'm a barrister. Mostly civil cases. Some constitutional stuff."

She gave voice to her suspicions about his background. "You're an Oxford man…Blaise."

He smiled, smoothing down his tie. "Yes. You recognize the tie. Captain of the rowing eight." He spread his arms wide and puffed out his chest. "Member of the Old Blues and Isis, though you wouldn't know it to look at me now."

Her heart did a strange flip. While it was true he'd probably gained weight, he was still broad-shouldered and well-muscled. The powers that be at Oxford didn't pick weaklings to captain their prestigious team. They chose leaders—strong men. "You look fit to me," she murmured into her wineglass, clenching the pulsating muscles between her legs.

It was getting uncomfortably hot in the restaurant. "Do you not have air conditioning?" she asked the waiter when he reappeared with the food.

He nodded to the floor-to-ceiling folding glass doors that had been opened to the street to relieve the July heat. "We don't switch it on when the doors are open," he replied with a barely concealed smirk and more than a trace of a Cockney accent. "Would you like to move closer to the outside?"

She shook her head, feeling like a fool, and he departed, no doubt rolling his eyes. This was getting out of hand. Time to get back to business. She sampled a tiny quail's egg, then said, "I've read some of your research."

He quickly swallowed the pizza he'd been chewing. "And?"

His voice sounded casual, but there was too much intensity in his unusual eyes. She was already certain that some of the information was flawed, but didn't yet know why it mattered so much to him. He didn't seem the type to care passionately about an anachronism like the *Sons of the Conquest*. "It's a rare treat to see hand-drawn family trees instead of computer-generated ones. You were right that your ancestor was meticulous."

He dabbed his mouth with the linen napkin, but missed a tiny spot of tomato sauce on his top lip. She had an insane urge to lick it off.

"But you have concerns," he said with a frown.

For a brief moment she was tempted to lie. Anything to wipe away the worry in his eyes. But she had her professional reputation to consider. She stared at the asparagus on her plate, her belly churning. "He relied heavily on some avenues of research that have since been proven unsupportable."

The color drained from his face and he stared at her as if she'd told him his best friend had died.

"I'm not saying your family isn't descended from a knight who fought at Hastings, I'm simply saying…"

"That it's not your area of expertise."

>>><<<

BLAISE GRITTED HIS teeth, cursing himself for a fool when Anne glared back angrily and thrust her fork into the remaining quail's egg like Saint George slaying the proverbial dragon.

A man in his profession never blurted out a judgmental statement of that sort. His emotions had got the better of him. The last thing he wanted to do was alienate the first woman he'd been attracted to in years. Plus, he was financially dependent on her goodwill. "I apologise," he muttered lamely.

She put down her knife and fork and stared at him. "Not that I have to justify my credentials to you, Mr. de

Wolfe, but it happens that the Norman Conquest *is* my area of expertise. I too am a descendant of a knight who fought at Hastings, the first Earl of Ellesmere, and what's more *I* can prove it."

Once again his better judgement failed him. "With a name like Smith?" he scoffed.

She crumpled her napkin and threw it onto the table. "I've changed my mind about the tiramisu," she said, pushing back her wheeled chair. "I trust you'll get this?"

She was gone before he could retract his accusation.

APOLOGIES

B LAISE DIDN'T WAIT for the bill. He grudgingly extracted thirty-five pounds from his wallet, figuring that would about cover it, and nodded impatiently to the money on the table when he caught the scowling waiter's eye. It wouldn't leave much of a tip after VAT, but what the hell. The pizza had as much texture and taste as cardboard and it was plain Anne hadn't enjoyed her food.

He hurried out and looked quickly up and down Gillinghall Street. Chances were she would walk back to her house only five minutes away.

He strode briskly to Belgrave Road, then took a left onto Eccleston Square, hoping to catch a glimpse of her, but was disappointed that she was nowhere in sight. Maybe she had taken a cab after all.

Halfway down the street he paused to take stock of the situation, shoving his hands into the pockets of his slacks. What was he going to say once he caught up with her? Would she even agree to carry on the research after his insult? For some inexplicable reason that no longer seemed to matter.

Drawn by the sound of rustling leaves in the Square's private gardens, he gripped the iron railings, feeling like a jailed outlaw in some old western. Discouraged, he looked across at the distant tennis court partly hidden by the London plane trees. A pulse throbbed wildly in his throat when he realized Anne was sitting on a bench a few yards away, staring at a glorious display of bedding out plants, looking lost and alone. An urgent compulsion to comfort her seized him.

He assumed she must have a key fob for the garden gate, available only to local residents. He had no choice but to ask her to let him in.

※※※※

ANNE HAD SOUGHT refuge in the locked garden, reasoning it would be better to avoid Blaise if he came in pursuit, but her heart skittered when he called her name. "Anne, let me in. I need to apologise properly."

She got up from the bench and went to the gate. "I don't want to argue," she told him through the railings.

"Neither do I," he replied, "and I'm sorry I was rude. It's not in my nature."

Despite the insult, there was genuine regret in his voice and she believed him. She unlocked the gate and walked back to the bench. He followed and sat beside her. She startled when his leg pressed against hers.

He took her hand. "What's wrong?"

How to tell him the warmth of his solid thigh was the most intimate contact she'd had with a male for years, and it felt wonderful. "No, and I'm sorry too for walking out like that. It was childish. Smith is my married name."

He meshed his fingers with hers. The strength in his touch gave her courage to tell the whole story, but even so her voice faltered. "I'm a widow. My husband was a career soldier. He died in Iraq."

Those were the facts, but she wasn't ready to pour out her grief and anger to a man she barely knew.

He put his arm around her shoulders. "How long ago?"

The urge to lean into him and accept his comfort was powerful, but she held herself aloof, otherwise she might dissolve into tears. She swallowed the lump in her throat. "Three years."

"And yet it seems like only yesterday."

She knew from the wistful resignation in his voice that he too had suffered a wrenching emotional loss. A sweetheart? A wife?

"I come here when things get too much," she whispered. "This garden saved my sanity after Geoff died. I was only a child when it was torn apart by the Great Storm of 1987, but my parents and I helped with the restoration."

"I've heard of that," he replied, tightening his grip on her shoulder. "One hundred mile an hour winds, right? We were spared the worst of it out in the country."

She gave in and leaned against him, feeling less tense than she'd felt in a long time. "Yes, we lost seven of the plane trees and all the railings were torn out. The machinery brought in to clear some of the debris chewed up the grass. It was devastating."

He rested his chin on the top of her head. "You'd never know by looking at it now. It's a beautiful new world."

GUILT

Anne may have misjudged this unlikely hero. Perhaps he was the knight in shining armor destined to ride to the rescue and carry her off to a beautiful new world of her own. He'd reawakened physical needs and yearnings. Much as she enjoyed delving into the past, she wanted a future, a life. "Would you like to come back to the house for a cup of tea?" she asked. "I guarantee the service is better than at Tazzi's."

"I'd like that," he replied in a deep voice that echoed in her bones. "We can start afresh."

They strolled hand in hand to St. George's Terrace and she unlocked the front door, feeling like a teenager on her first date.

"This is a beautiful property," he said as she ushered him into the hallway. "Are you the bike rider?"

"Yes, I find it handy for short errands, though I don't venture out on it at peak times. I'm glad you like the house," she added truthfully, leading the way up the stairs to the kitchen, deliberately exaggerating the sway of her hips.

When she and Geoff hosted dinner parties, guests were always awed by the ultra-modern brilliant white decor and stainless steel appliances. She'd forgotten how proud she used to be of the gleaming space. Blaise's *Wow!* lifted her spirits and brought back good memories.

"Have a seat and I'll put on the kettle."

"Counter or kitchen table?" he asked.

Contentment washed over her. "The table's fine."

After plugging in the electric kettle, she opened the cupboard and dithered over which mugs to use. She had her favorite Royal Doulton, but men didn't drink out of china. Geoff preferred a plain…

She gritted her teeth and grabbed two china mugs. Blaise belonged to the landed gentry. Didn't they all drink tea from the finest china, stirred with a silver spoon? "Milk and sugar?" she asked, trying to slow her breathing.

"Just milk," he replied, patting his stomach. "Have to cut down."

Waiting for the kettle to boil, she drummed her

fingers on the counter, not sure why she resented people like Blaise when she herself had noble ancestors.

He stood behind her chair and pulled it out when she brought the tea tray, but she hesitated before sitting down.

"What is it?" he asked.

She clutched the back of the chair. "I know it's silly, but I haven't used this table since my husband died."

He held out his hand. "I understand, and I'm honored to be your first guest."

She might disdain the upper class, but Blaise was obviously a gentleman. She took his hand. His strength became her strength and she sat.

"I'll let it steep for a few minutes," she told him, anxious to fill the silence.

"I meant it when I said I understand," he replied, staring at the checkered tablecloth. "I was engaged a few years ago. After we broke up I avoided restaurants where we'd eaten together, didn't go to shows at theatres we frequented." He smiled nervously as she poured his tea. "Her name was Tessa."

She got the feeling it was an effort for him to even say the woman's name. "I take it she ended the relationship?"

He nodded. "I couldn't sleep in the bed we shared, not even in the same room. I moved to another bedchamber." He flashed a wry smile. "It's not as though De Wolfe Hall is short of them."

She propped both elbows on the table and sipped her tea, glad she'd invited him. "I'm imagining a grand mansion with acres and acres of manicured grounds."

He narrowed his eyes and clenched his jaw. Something had changed. "Enough about me," he growled. "Tell me about your husband."

She curled her hands around the bone china mug hoping its heat would dull the pain of having to put her grief into words.

⟫⟫⟪⟪

IT HAD BEEN on the tip of Blaise's tongue to disclose why Tessa left him, but he thought better of it. No point in letting Anne know yet that he faced financial challenges. "Take your time," he assured her as she squirmed in her seat, holding on to the gold-rimmed china mug like a shipwreck survivor clings to a piece of driftwood.

She stared at some spot on the wall behind him. "While Geoff was away in Iraq on his first tour of duty

I was a nervous wreck. He was older than me and a career soldier when I met him. I should have been prepared, but I was so swept up in the excitement of being married to a handsome officer, it never occurred to me he might be sent into a war zone. It was an overwhelming relief when he came home, not only safe, but a decorated hero. Most of our social life revolved around the military and everywhere we went people congratulated him for his bravery. I was very proud and thankful."

She sipped her tea and he let her take her time.

"But he was restless. Something was bothering him. He became moody, flying off the handle at the least thing. Being around him was like walking on eggs. When he refused to discuss it, I stopped asking and spent most of my time on my research. We lived in the same house, but we became strangers."

She stared into the empty cup.

He reached for the teapot handle. "Refill?"

She focussed on the golden liquid as he poured. "He came home drunk one evening and told me at this bloody table that he'd volunteered to go back to Iraq weeks before."

His heart went out to her. Tessa's devastating betrayal suddenly seemed insignificant. "No wonder you don't sit here."

She smiled weakly. "I don't remember much of what happened after that. I yelled and cried a lot. Accused him of not loving me. Threw things. I didn't even see him off when he shipped out a week later."

She rocked back and forth, gripping the edges of her chair. His analytical skills kicked in. "And you feel guilty about that because he came home in a box."

She looked at him as if he'd said the moon was made of green cheese. "An improvised explosive device detonated next to him and he was blown to bits." She swallowed hard. "I do feel guilty but it's because part of me thought it served him right. He left me when he didn't have to. I couldn't compete with a godforsaken country in the back of beyond."

She clenched her fists and brought them down hard on the tabletop. Tears trickled down her cheeks. "I never said goodbye."

He got out of his chair, pulled her up against him and cradled her in his arms as she sobbed.

※

ANNE HAD NEVER known what it was to be comforted

by a man. Blaise's solid strength was an anchor in a sea of loneliness in which she'd floundered for too long—perhaps even since before her marriage. Geoff had no patience for *weakness*. The tears gradually turned to heavy sighs that eventually became hiccups.

He reached over to retrieve a box of tissues from the counter. "You might need these."

She pulled out a wad and blew her nose. She must look a fright, but he kept their bodies locked together, his arms around her waist. It was impossible not to be aware of the hard maleness pressed against her. "I'm sorry. I don't know what came over me," she murmured.

"A good cry is cathartic," he replied with a smile, rubbing her upper arms as he eased away. She missed his warmth instantly.

"Now, lead the way to the parlor. You should relax and put your feet up."

"I have work to do for an important client," she protested weakly.

He put an arm around her waist and forced her to walk to the door. "Later."

Glad to have someone else make a decision for her, she obeyed with only feigned resistance and led the way, embarrassed when he noticed his grandfather's papers scattered on the carpet. "They fell off my lap," she explained. "I meant to pick them up, but…"

He sat her down on the couch then gathered up the research and leafed his thumb through the pile before putting it on the armchair. "You read quite a bit."

"Yes," she replied sheepishly. "But let's not talk about that now."

He sat beside her, leaned back into the corner and gathered her into his arms. "I agree. I'll have to leave in half an hour for my meeting, but I'd like to just hold you, if that's okay."

She laid her head on his chest and put her feet up on the couch. Difficulties lay ahead, but for the moment she was content to lie in his warm embrace and listen to the steady thud of his heart. The guilt she'd held inside for too long seemed to have lost its power over her.

<hr />

AFTER TESSA'S MATTER-OF-FACT declaration that she couldn't possibly marry a man who didn't have the means to provide for her in the manner she'd expected, Blaise buried himself in his work.

He often worked through lunch, preferring to spend his time with paperwork than face the outside world of restaurants and cafeterias. He fell into the habit of staying late at the office, only leaving in time to catch the last train home to Surrey. De Wolfe Hall was the reason he'd lost the love of his life. The less time he spent there the better.

Colleagues suggested women they knew that he might take out, and he eventually agreed. He took various attractive and intelligent women to lunch, to the theatre, the cinema, even on one occasion up the Thames on a riverboat from Westminster to Hampton Court Palace—possibly the longest four hours of his life.

He itched for every date to be over. He found he had nothing to talk to them about. It wasn't a surprise when they politely declined his half-hearted attempts to arrange another *date.* If pushed, he might be able to recall their names. He remembered more of the interesting trivia he'd learned about Henry VIII and his magnificent palace from the guided tour.

He looked down at Anne's blonde head resting on his chest and marveled that he felt at ease with her. At least his heart was at ease. His cock was standing to attention. She'd resurrected urges and needs he'd feared Tessa had killed stone cold dead.

He toyed with the idea of cupping Anne's tempting breast but thought better of it. Too soon, and in any case he'd stopped carrying condoms.

He rubbed his thumb along the stubble on his chin. Difficulties lay ahead. He'd have to be forthcoming about his financial situation. He thought he'd been honest with Tessa, but apparently she'd only heard what she wanted to hear, and admittedly he'd spent money he could ill afford on courting her.

Opening that can of worms would inevitably bring up the restoration grant he'd been *guaranteed* by the president of the *Sons of the Conquest*, who happened to be his boss.

If he succeeded in becoming a member.

Anne was the key to that. She'd hinted there might be problems with the research, but surely that didn't mean he wasn't a descendant of Sir Gaetan? The entire de Wolfe family history was predicated on that belief. His view of himself and the world he lived in depended on it being true.

Suspecting she'd nodded off, he reluctantly eased himself off the couch, tucked a cushion under her head and left for his appointment.

ANNE TURNED OVER on the couch and stared at the crown molding, listening to the *thwack, thwack* of tennis balls. Someone was using the courts over in the gardens. It must have cooled off outside while she slept.

She hugged the cushion, content that she'd been comfortable enough with Blaise to fall asleep in his arms. She hadn't even heard him leave.

She sat up and stretched, filled with an exciting premonition that a relationship with him held promise. She was a butterfly emerging from the cocoon of loneliness and resentment.

Time to leave the past behind.

But then she remembered he was a client who was expecting great things from her, though she didn't understand why, and she already had serious misgivings about his research. Something was missing, but she couldn't put her finger on what it was.

However, she wouldn't find the answer by lounging around the parlor.

She got to her feet, retrieved the de Wolfe papers and went to her office.

DINNER FOR TWO

AT THREE O'CLOCK the next day Anne signed out of the prestigious library at the Society of Genealogists after spending several hours trying to verify some aspects of the de Wolfe family history.

The roar of the noisy London traffic came as a shock after the silent sanctity of the library.

She eventually flagged down a taxi on Goswell Street and settled in for the twenty minute ride back to St. George's Terrace. Turning on her mobile, she discovered Blaise had left her a text message earlier in the afternoon.

Hi Anne. Dinner 2nite?

Anticipation zinged. He'd never been far from her thoughts as she delved into his lineage and had been hoping he would call. She added his number to her contacts and called him back.

"De Wolfe."

His gruff manner took her by surprise. "Er, it's

Anne. Sorry it's taken me so long to reply. I was in a library and mobiles aren't allowed."

"I was afraid you were avoiding me."

His warmer tone settled her nerves. She was beginning to crave his company, but it was too soon to admit that, even to herself. "No. But I have a better idea. I'll cook dinner for us."

"Are you sure?"

His surprise was genuine and he sounded almost relieved.

"Yes. It will be more intimate." That wasn't what she'd intended to say. "I mean we can discuss my progress on your research without any interruptions. I think you'll be happy with what I found."

"I like the sound of *intimate*," he replied, the deep timbre of his voice causing a warm tingling to blossom and spread from her thighs to her nipples.

"Five, five-thirty," she stammered, casting an anxious glance at the cab driver's rear view mirror. His attention was on the road and thankfully he didn't seem to have noticed she'd melted into a seething mass of sexual desire.

Having spent the day researching medieval documents, a thought sprang to mind. "Wanton woman," she declared.

The cabbie cocked back his head. "*Wot*, miss?"

※※※

AT FIVE MINUTES to five, Blaise rang Anne's doorbell bubbling with an anticipation he hadn't felt in years. He chuckled at the realization he didn't care a whit that he'd accomplished nothing all day at the office, totally preoccupied with seeing her again.

He clutched the beautifully wrapped and beribboned yellow carnations, reasonably confident she wouldn't suspect he'd almost had a heart attack when the florist told him the price of a dozen roses.

"I'm in the kitchen," she called after the lock buzzed open.

Bursting with energy, he took the stairs two at a time and handed her the flowers when she greeted him shyly with a peck on the cheek. "How did you know I love carnations? I have no luck with roses. They wilt as soon as they see me."

He shrugged, comfortable with the lie he was about to tell. "I just knew."

She propped the flowers in the corner of the sink, went to the cupboard and reached up for a vase. Her shapely bottom and long legs stirred interest at his groin. He came up behind her and put his hands on her hips, elated when she pushed back against his arousal. He folded his arms around her, relishing the swell of her breasts on his forearms. "You tempt me," he whispered.

She covered his arms with hers. Her purr of contentment when he nibbled her outstretched neck pushed him over the edge and his hips took on a life of their own.

"I've thought about kissing you all day," she murmured.

He turned her to face him and bent his head. She opened readily to his coaxing and their tongues mated. He trailed his fingertips along her neck, savoring the warm taste of woman, inhaling a delicate perfume he couldn't name mingled with the alluring scent of an aroused female.

She raked her fingers through his hair, came up on her toes and pressed her pelvis to his needy cock.

An angry hissing sound broke them apart when something boiled over on the stove. She hurried to remove the pan from the element. "Shit!"

Indeed, his throbbing dick echoed.

"Everything is nearly ready," she said, her face beet red. "Just have to mash these potatoes. I hope you like chicken."

"I do, and I'm ravenously hungry," he replied as she drained the pan into a colander.

He was disappointed when she didn't rise to the bait. "Good. We'll eat in the dining room and I'll tell you about my research, then maybe later…"

He arched his brows, encouraged by her seductive smile. "Maybe later I can do some in-depth research of my own."

>>><<<

INVITING BLAISE TO eat in the formal dining room tested Anne's mettle. She'd probably overdone it with the gold-plated cutlery, damask tablecloth and Irish crystal, but this was after all an occasion to celebrate.

She placed the china plates on the teak table and he held out her chair as she sat. "Smells delicious," he remarked with a sly smile, his eyes fixed on hers.

She picked up the bottle of wine, her tummy doing strange fluttery things. "Malbec?"

He held out his glass. "Waterford," he exclaimed. "We used to have the same pattern, but…"

A sadness crept into his eyes as his voice trailed off, but then he clinked his glass against hers. "My father reserved the Waterford for V.I.P.s."

"You are a special guest," she admitted, her eyes darting around the room.

He followed her gaze. "Let me guess, you haven't used this room for three years."

She sipped her wine. "Right again, now eat before it gets cold."

"Yes, mum," he teased. "Tell me what you've unearthed."

My heart. My desires. My life.

But her hopes might all come crashing down around her ears. "Your grandfather made some errors, not surprising given the lack of resources at the time, but overall his research is solid."

He stopped chewing, the relief evident in his jewelled eyes. "So the de Wolfes are descended from true Normans?"

She should keep her reservations to herself and simply endorse his application. She chewed her bottom lip. "There is no doubt you are a descendant of Gaetan de Wolfe."

He sipped his wine, then filled his mouth with

another forkful, chewing happily.

She hesitated. "And Gaetan did accompany the Conqueror to England. His name is on the list of William's companions that sits above the door of the church in Dives-sur-mer."

He grinned. "I've heard of that, but I've never seen it. Maybe some day you can take me to see where the invasion kicked off."

The notion of travelling through Normandy with him, visiting places of great historical significance, was more than appealing, but he might not want to see her again after she was done. "My Norman ancestor was the man who compiled the muster role," she murmured, hesitant to mention the Montbryce name. "I discovered that piece of information in the family annals begun by the fourth Earl of Ellesmere. They were donated to the Shropshire Archives in Shrewsbury."

"Really. Maybe our ancestors knew each other."

"Probably," she confirmed, getting the distinct feeling he was only half listening. "They both fought at Hastings and were granted earldoms in recognition of their service to King William."

His eyes widened. "Gaetan was made an earl?"

"Of Wolverhampton," she replied.

He raised his glass. "To the conquering heroes of Hastings."

She'd never heard of anyone's grip snapping the stem of a Waterford wineglass, but feared she might set the precedent. There was just one more thing to verify, but if she told him he might not take her to bed.

HUNGRY WOLF

BLAISE HAD AN urge to strut around the dining room thumping his chest. Everything was going to work out. The substantial grant from the *Sons of the Conquest* was his. De Wolfe Hall would be saved. The icing on the cake was that he'd found a wonderful woman. He had a very good feeling about the future of his relationship with Anne Smith.

He finished every last morsel of his dinner, enjoying the first meal in a long time he hadn't eaten with his gut in knots. "You're a good cook," he said between mouthfuls. "But you've hardly touched yours."

She shrugged, laying down her knife and fork. "I'm not very hungry."

He put her obvious hesitation down to nervousness, sensing she knew as well as he did that the evening was going to end in the bedroom. The condoms were in his blazer pocket. The little swimmers in his balls were already on the move.

She gathered the dishes, got up and took them into the kitchen. He was tempted to follow, but decided to allow her some time to settle her nerves. He didn't want to give the impression he was a randy wolf on the prowl.

He chuckled at his own joke.

A hungry de Wolfe!

A classic Duran Duran song drifted into his thoughts. *Hungry like the wolf.* He whistled the first few bars.

"You're a good whistler," Anne said as she reappeared carrying what looked like a large bowl of trifle. "That's a Duran Duran song isn't it? They are one of my all-time favorite bands. Can I tempt you with dessert?"

※※※※

ANNE WANTED TO bite her tongue. Regaining her seat, she looked away from the unmistakable fire in Blaise's eyes that she'd ignited without meaning to. Or maybe she had.

Perhaps her desire to sleep with him had taken control of her brain, but there was the nagging matter of verifying one last detail about Gaetan de Wolfe. Was it something she'd read long ago in the Montbryce papers? "Sorry. That sounded rather suggestive," she quipped lamely, brandishing the serving spoon.

Blaise took the utensil and lay it on the table, then reached for her hands. She hoped the trembling tying her tummy in knots wasn't obvious to him. If he asked why she was afraid she wouldn't be able to explain it.

She wanted him. He drew her in a way Geoff never had. She'd loved her husband, but just looking at Blaise was like a blow to the solar plexus. Her hormones were getting the better of her. Maybe she'd been too long without sex.

But if they embarked on an intimate relationship with something unspoken between them…

He stroked his thumbs along the backs of her hands. "I want you, Anne," he rasped.

The need in his deep voice convinced her she was overcomplicating things, not for the first time in her life. They were both consenting adults. "I want you too," she whispered, twirling her thumb across his palm.

⁂

ANNE TOOK BLAISE'S hand and led him up another

flight of stairs to her bedroom.

His impression was that it was just as tastefully furnished and decorated as the rest of the house, but he was too preoccupied with other thoughts to pay attention.

He'd come close to absent-mindedly removing his blazer and leaving it in the dining room, which would have left him up the creek without a paddle—make that up in the bedroom without a condom!

It didn't matter now that he hadn't told Anne of his financial woes. It was fitting that her expertise had saved his bacon.

He shoved aside comments from Tessa that he'd never given much thought to before, mildly perplexed that memories of her half-hearted response in bed would resurface now.

But the fire burning in his veins for Anne was far more intense than anything he'd ever felt for Tessa. How he'd ever believed himself in love with the faithless cow...

Love?

Was he falling in love with Anne? Did she feel anything for him? He took off his blazer and gathered her into his arms, knowing without a doubt that he was the first man to enter this bedroom in three years. It flashed into his mind that she'd removed her wedding ring. It gave him hope. She didn't fight him, but she was tense. "It's okay, sweetheart," he reassured her. "I'm a little out of practice myself."

She nodded, fiddling with his tie. "I don't want you to be disappointed. I was never much good in bed."

A notion flitted into his subconscious that Geoff Smith and Tessa Mulberry would have made a perfect couple. All take and no give. "Undress for me," he rasped. "I want to see all of you."

Her already heated face turned a lovely shade of pink, but she looked like the proverbial deer in the headlights. He swore to kill Captain Smith if he ever met him. Oh, wait! The bastard was dead.

He untangled her arms from his neck and eased her away, hoping his smile would give her confidence. "Strip for me."

She flared her nostrils and stretched her neck. The pleasant reaction in his balls warned that going slow might not be such a good idea.

She unbuttoned the waistband of her skirt and shimmied the garment off her hips. It pooled at her feet and she kicked it away, wobbling on high heels. He thought tights had replaced suspenders and stockings, but he was wrong and his throbbing cock scolded him for his ignorance. "Christ, Anne," he growled in a voice he barely recognised as he hurriedly unbuckled his belt.

Seemingly emboldened by his drooling, she turned her back to him and thrust out her bottom. The stockings had diverted his attention from the black thong. He couldn't help but notice it now. Though the show wasn't over, he had to put his hands on her cheeks. "You're beautiful," he whispered.

She purred when he traced a finger along the sheer fabric that barely covered her rosette.

He stepped back, praying he could stay the course without stalking and devouring her like Duran Duran's hungry wolf. "Breasts now."

Once the blouse was unbuttoned and cast aside, she hesitated and looked at him warily. He licked his lips, awestruck at the bounty that swelled in the confines of her lacy black bra.

It was his duty as a gentleman to help her clear the final hurdle. He slipped the straps off her shoulders and cupped her breasts, lifting them, relishing their delicious weight.

She reached behind to undo the hooks, arching her

back when he brushed his thumbs over the rigid nipples. When she pressed her hand to his rock hard arousal, Tarzan's call of the jungle echoed in the back of his mind. However, if he bellowed out his triumph he wouldn't be able to suckle the pale nipples, and that was his more immediate need.

She seemed to find her confidence as he suckled and before he knew it his trousers were round his ankles and she was lifting him out of his boxers.

"Clever girl," he growled, moving his fingers to the sliver of fabric between her legs. "You're already wet for me."

But then it occurred to his fevered brain she was having some difficulty extracting him from his underwear. "You're big," she murmured apologetically.

Now his conundrum was how to strut like a rooster, thump his chest like a gorilla, be shuck of the boxers and thong and thrust into her wet heat before his cock exploded.

He shoved the underwear down over his hips, stepped out of them and the trousers at the same time, and scooped her up.

He perched her on the edge of the bed and parted her legs. His need was urgent but he had to taste her first. He peeled off the thong and stared at the moist pink heaven that would soon welcome him. He fell to his knees on the carpet, parted her outer lips with his thumbs and sucked her juices like a man who has wandered in the desert and finally stumbled upon the hidden oasis.

Her sweet nub swelled beneath his tongue. He clamped his arms around her thighs as she writhed and moaned. She raked her fingers through his hair, called his name over and over, until she dug her nails into his forearms and keened out a long, slow release.

She suddenly fell silent, and he worried she had passed out, or stopped breathing, or both, but then she spread her legs wider and in the sexiest, sultriest voice he'd ever heard said, "Come inside. Now."

He got to his feet and rushed to retrieve the condom from his blazer, wondering why the hell he hadn't had the foresight to have it ready. The trembling in his hands made it difficult to tear open the packet. "I'm out of practice with these fucking things," he yelled.

She smiled like a woman who's just had a great orgasm. "I'll help while you take off your shirt and tie."

Anne had never understood Geoff's insistence on condoms. Having children was something he always promised to discuss *later*. They had plenty of time.

Except time had run out for him, and here she was smoothing a condom onto an engorged penis that could only be described as *magnificent*.

Geoff took care of himself and she hoped Blaise hadn't sensed it was the first time she'd ever attempted the task.

She wasn't too worried as he stood with legs braced, breathing heavily, watching her handiwork. He was lost in a testosterone laden world, humming an off-key version of *Hungry Like the Wolf* deep in his throat, and it hadn't occurred to him he still wore his shirt and tie.

Her inner muscles pulsed on the glow from the mind-boggling orgasm.

When she declared the sheathing complete, he raked his hair off his face, stalked onto the bed on all fours, lifted her hips and settled himself between her legs.

MADNESS

BLAISE PAUSED FOR a fraction of a second, tempted to ask Anne if he might remove the condom, though he had to admit he'd never enjoyed being sheathed quite so much.

He felt her heat, but she was in his blood and he wanted to touch her intimately without the latex between them.

However, the expectancy in her glazed eyes indicated she couldn't wait any longer either, so he tabled the discussion for another time, and thrust.

She held her breath and whimpered. He supposed there must be some discomfort when a woman hadn't had sex for three years, so he somehow found the wherewithal to hold still. "Are you okay?"

She nodded. "As you said. Out of practice…but don't stop."

Relieved, he withdrew until he was at her opening then thrust again, more slowly, deeply. She put her hands on his chest and clenched her inner muscles on him.

He liked it so much he did it again, then she matched him stroke for stroke as madness took over. He plundered and took, suckled and kissed, babbling like a maniac until she screamed out his name when she climaxed again. He pumped and pumped, draining the last drop of seed from his body. Unlikely and absurd as it was, he half-hoped the condom had failed and they'd made a child.

Exhausted but supremely happy, he collapsed on top of her, his head full of images of healthy toddlers with curly blonde hair.

It was a few minutes before he realized he was drooling on her neck. He raised himself up on his forearms. "Sorry. Too heavy."

She looked sleepily content. "I didn't mind your weight."

"You're still clenching on me," he said.

She smiled. "It's involuntary. You got me all excited."

His sated cock slid from her body and curled up in the warm nest it had made for itself. "That was the idea."

Anne stretched her arms above her head, wishing they hadn't had to use a condom. She shivered when Blaise lifted off her and lay on his side, one arm bent to support his head. He put his arm around her and drew her back into his warmth. She nuzzled her nose in the soft dusting of dark hair on his broad chest.

She wanted to tell him it was the most exhilarating sexual experience she'd ever had, but his satisfied grin indicated she might have screamed words to that effect at the height of her euphoria.

She listened to his breathing, to the steady thud of his heartbeat and knew she was in trouble. Now she'd found this man, how could she risk losing him? The future never held any guarantees but her body and her heart told her Blaise was the right partner for her.

She wasn't sure how long they lay together when he checked his watch. "Much as I hate to kiss and run, the last train to Virginia Water leaves Waterloo at ten to eleven."

His yawn told her he'd prefer to spend the night. But that wasn't possible. "How long does it take?"

He hesitated, then said, "Half an hour to forty

minutes. My car is parked at the station and it's another ten minute drive home."

She made a show of checking the bedside clock. "So if you leave now you'll have plenty of time to make it to Waterloo Station."

He removed his arm and sat up with his back to her, his arms around his bent knees. She'd disappointed him and wanted to make amends. "I have to get up early in the morning," she explained.

Her heart lurched at the confusion in his eyes when he turned to look at her. "Why?"

"I'm taking the 8 o'clock train to Wolverhampton."

He smirked. "Why would you want to go…"

The moment the reason dawned on him, she toyed with abandoning any further digging into the past.

"I thought you said you'd verified everything and were ready to sign off on the research."

Avoiding his angry gaze, she slid off the bed and retrieved her robe from the back of the bathroom door. "No," she replied, swallowing the lump in her throat, "I said you were definitely descended from Sir Gaetan."

He got to his feet as she tied the belt of her robe, then his face reddened when he glanced at the condom. "Just a minute," he growled, disappearing into the bathroom, boxers in hand.

She sat on the edge of the bed, her heart in knots, listening to the sound of running water. Professional ethics were pushing her to track down Gaetan de Wolfe's parentage, but integrity wouldn't warm her bed, wouldn't lift her to the heights of bliss.

She stood when he emerged from the bathroom several minutes later. "Please don't be angry."

He retrieved his trousers and pulled them on over his boxers. "You couldn't tell me this before we slept together?" he hissed.

He grabbed his shirt and tie when she handed them to him and pulled away when she tried to help him button the shirt. "I don't understand why you're so angry. Does it really matter if your application is rejected?"

He looked at her as if she'd lost her mind, then sat on the edge of the bed to slip on his loafers. "You obviously don't get it," he spat.

He picked up his blazer and headed for the stairs. She heard the door slam as he left the house.

He was right. She didn't get it and her confusion only added to her heartbreak.

BLAISE WEDGED HIMSELF into a second class seat on the commuter train to Virginia Water, gripped the arms and took a deep breath. Getting from Pimlico to Waterloo had taken a half hour of walking and changing stations twice on the Tube. There'd been no time to think, to analyze what had happened.

One minute he'd been buried deep in a moist sheath, his happy cock held in the warm pulsating grip of a woman he was falling in love with. Next minute she'd betrayed him. Did she not realize what was riding on his acceptance into the *Sons of the Conquest*?

The train pulled out of the station and the steady clickety-clack of steel on steel gradually helped slow his frantic heartbeat and dull the ache at his temples. As they picked up speed, outlines of buildings loomed from the darkness then were gone. Blurred street lights flashed by, level crossing sirens wailed, moonlight shimmered on waterways.

He dozed off, but reality suddenly hit home and he was wide awake. He pinched the bridge of his nose. How could she know when he'd never told her? She probably thought he wanted to join for the prestige.

As if!

And still she'd wanted to sleep with him!

Once more he had let his emotions get the better of him. Now he would have to explain to her why it was vitally important his application be accepted.

If she ever agreed to see him again.

EXPLOSIVE INFORMATION

ANNE WAS UP and dressed well before the alarm went off at five the next morning. While filling the dishwasher after the ill-fated dinner before going to bed she'd come to the unwelcome conclusion that acceptance into the *Sons of the Conquest* was more than a passing fancy for Blaise. For some reason it was vitally important to him, and he wanted it desperately enough to sleep with the researcher he thought could make it happen.

Trying unsuccessfully to fathom his motives had kept her awake most of the night, but of one thing she was certain. She'd been a fool to think a man like him would be interested in a woman with so much emotional baggage.

She'd already booked and paid for the train ticket on line, but what was the point now of going all the way to Wolverhampton? A long list of less complicated projects awaited her attention. She could make up some excuse to cancel the appointment she'd made at the Archives. Blaise would most likely turn the project over to some other, less ethical genealogist in order to get what he wanted.

But, damn it, she didn't have it in her to leave something important unfinished, and then there was the nagging inkling that there was more to Gaetan de Wolfe's story. She'd learned over the years that when it came to breaking down brick walls in family tree research, you often had to trust your hunches.

She resolved to go to Wolverhampton and see the commission through to completion, whatever the end result. If Blaise chose not to accept her findings and refused to pay the fee, so be it. She'd learned her lesson. Evidently, he wasn't her knight in shining armor. The probability stung like a slap in the face.

After a quick breakfast of some tasteless cereal at the counter, she gathered the materials she needed, stretching an elastic band around a handful of sharpened pencils. Pens weren't allowed in most county record offices and she doubted the Wolverhampton Archives would be any different. She hefted the computer bag over her shoulder, left the house and hailed a cab.

"Euston Station, please," she told the cabbie after climbing in the back.

"Righto, miss!"

The express train left on time, and less than two hours later, she glanced up at the clock as she exited Wolverhampton Station. If asked, she could describe the intricate designs made by raindrops across the carriage window, but had no idea of the cities and towns she'd traveled through.

According to Google Maps, the Archives were only a short cab ride away on Whitmore Hill and she'd be there in good time for her appointment at ten o'clock. She'd explained her area of interest to the archivist in a telephone call and hoped pertinent documents had been found for her to peruse.

She presented her identification to a grey-haired docent of indeterminate age. Sylvia gushed an enthusiastic Black Country greeting. "Alrite, Bab? You've had a journey."

She smiled in reply, appreciative of the warm welcome.

Sylvia issued her a pair of nitrile gloves and led the way to a research cubicle. Clearly the woman had looked forward to her arrival. It boded well.

"If people don't find what they're looking for here," Sylvia explained, "they go to Stafford. It's only fifteen minutes by rail and the trains run frequently."

That made sense, since Wolverhampton was formerly in the county of Staffordshire before the counties were reorganized in 1975. "Thank you. I appreciate that, but I didn't make an appointment there."

She hadn't planned on having to go to Stafford, but if that's what it took…

The guide leaned over conspiratorially. "I don't think you'll be going to Stafford."

It seemed the woman had found something she thought would be of interest. Her hands suddenly felt too hot in the nitrile gloves. "Let's see what you've got," she said, eyeing the documents spread out on the display table with a sense of anticipation only another researcher would comprehend.

Sylvia lay a loving gloved hand on one of the scrolled parchments. "I might suggest starting here. Can you read Latin, or do you need me to assist?"

She cringed. "I was afraid of that. I have A-Level Latin, and I've done similar research, but I'm out of practice."

The blue eyes lit up. "Well, then," she said, "this is

an account of the battle of Wellesbourne written by Antillius Decimus Rubrum."

Anne wheeled a chair up to the table. "And he was?"

"A Briton descended from members of an ancient Roman legion. His people still spoke Latin at the time of the Norman Conquest."

"Gosh, and I thought I knew all there was to know about eleventh century Britain."

Sylvia preened. "Antillius helped the Normans in their struggle to subdue the Mercians."

"But I understood Gaetan de Wolfe married a Mercian princess after he became Earl of Wolverhampton."

Sylvia carefully unrolled part of the parchment. "He did. Her name was Ghislaine. She was the sister of Edwin of Mercia." She pointed to a line of script that looked like hieroglyphics. "It's all here. *Gislayn uxor Gaetanis*, with the date, but that's hard to make out exactly."

Anne peered at the ancient writing Sylvia pointed out. "I see."

"Antillius was very thorough. It was a Roman trait you know. He's even given the details of Gaetan's parentage."

Anne's heart lurched. Here was the point of no return. The woman in love warred with the professional researcher, all the while knowing in her heart which would inevitably win. She pulled her chair closer, peering at the indecipherable script.

Sylvia glowed. "Look. Here. *Gaetan filius bastardus Daciae mulier nobilis ab Vasconia et militis Normanorum.*"

One word hit Anne between the eyes. "He was a bastard?"

"Yes, Antillius explains he was the illegitimate son of Dacia, a noblewoman from Gascony, and a Norman knight. Very common occurrence, of course, in medieval times."

Anne's hopes of a reconciliation with Blaise had been tenuous at best. This explosive information that Gaetan's unwed mother was not a Norman doomed any chance of a future together. It was a triumph worthy of a Greek tragedy.

EUSTON STATION

BLAISE WAS UP at the crack of dawn, pacing the Long Gallery built into the roof of De Wolfe Hall. It was an architectural marvel that ran the length of the house, but he'd sold off most of the furniture and area rugs, leaving only the wide planked flooring. Still, it afforded a grand view of the estate and was a place he came when his worries threatened to get the better of him. It was where he'd eventually overcome his fear of heights.

All through breakfast, he hoped Anne might call before she left for the Midlands, but knew in his heart she wouldn't. She was a proud woman and he'd hurt her. She probably thought he'd enticed her into bed to ensure she gave him a favorable pedigree.

He contemplated not going into the office, but at least there he had stuff to occupy him.

His normally dependable car wouldn't start and he had to get the gardener to give him a boost. This caused him to miss his usual train into the city, and it was Murphy's Law that he bumped into his boss in the lobby of his firm's offices.

Maltravers had arrived early for once, tapping his watch as if Blaise was a naughty boy who had to be reminded of the importance of being on time. He was tempted to retort that he often put in hours, even days of unpaid overtime when arguing and researching a case. His success had earned the firm a great deal of money and he deserved to have been made a full partner eons ago, but there was no point antagonizing the old fool at this crucial time.

"My office," Maltravers croaked menacingly.

Irritated at being summoned like a clerk, Blaise followed him down the hall to the sumptuously decorated corner office that put his own to shame. "Don't forget the deadline," his boss declared, not even inviting him to sit. Evidently this wasn't to be a social chat.

How could he forget? He clasped his hands together behind his back, lest he be tempted to strangle the pompous demagogue. "Yes, sir. One more week."

Not a religious man, he nevertheless prayed Anne wouldn't dig up anything that might put his grant in peril. He imagined the smug satisfaction on his boss's face if he wasn't accepted into the *Sons*. He sometimes wondered if he'd been set up for failure. One of the agents acting on behalf of mainland Chinese buyers had inadvertently let slip a connection with Maltravers.

He was dismissed with a grunt and a wave of the hand as the supercilious man eased his corpulent girth into the black leather chair.

Blaise went to his office and made an effort to concentrate on his work, but late in the afternoon found himself googling *Earl of Wolverhampton*, and *Gaetan de Wolfe*, and then *Anne Smith*. The latter turned up a million results but then he narrowed it to *Anne Smith Genealogist*, and discovered just how respected she was in her field. She was sometimes referred to as Anne Bryce-Smith and he supposed Bryce was her maiden name. There was mention of her husband, and that led him into various glowing accounts of the captain's bravery and heroic self-sacrifice. "Bastard," he hissed.

Having learned nothing new from searching his ancestor, he googled train schedules for Wolverhampton to London, verified that the terminus was Euston Station, switched off his computer and left.

ANNE WAS EXHAUSTED and sick at heart by the time her train pulled in to Euston. It was no surprise she alighted on Platform 13.

As the miles sped by, she'd tried convincing herself that the information about Gaetan de Wolfe was so obscure no one was ever likely to find out if she certified that Blaise's conquering ancestor was of pure Norman extraction.

But she would know and the fear of being found out and the falsehood discovered would haunt her. It was impossible, especially since she didn't understand why it was so important to Blaise.

There was the added complication of her own birthright. Concealing the truth would be a betrayal of Ram de Montbryce, First Earl of Ellesmere. The compulsion to honor the memory of an ancestor who'd died more than nine hundred years before would seem silly to most people, but her roots represented everything she stood for.

She checked her watch as she followed the stream of passengers into the main concourse and glanced up to verify it with the station clock. She saw Blaise standing under the giant display a second or two before he saw her. The hundreds of commuters blurred into the background as they stared at each other.

Her frantically beating heart's desire was to rush into his arms and tell him she'd found nothing in Wolverhampton. But she'd never been a liar and what did the future hold for a relationship built on a lie? She'd been there, done that.

She squared her shoulders and tightened her grip on the strap of her laptop bag as he came towards her. He didn't look angry, which was perhaps reassuring, and he'd obviously sought her out.

They came face to face. There was no point delaying the inevitable. "We need to talk," she said.

⇢⇢⇢⇠⇠⇠

THE BLEAK DETERMINATION in Anne's eyes, the rigid set of her shoulders, the thrust of her defiant chin, all confirmed Blaise's fear that De Wolfe Hall was lost.

There were a million things he wanted to say.

He understood.

Sleeping with her had been the most fulfilling sexual experience he'd ever had.

He loved her.

But he was afraid he'd lost her forever, and that loomed as a bigger catastrophe than having to sell his ancestral home. "There's Ed's Easy Diner across the piazza," he offered lamely.

She grimaced. "I'm not really in the mood for all that bright red upholstery, juke box music and formica table tops. I had a snack on the train."

It was a relief in a way because he needed to hold her and soothe away the lines of worry. He decided to take a chance. "Come with me to De Wolfe Hall," he suggested, taking her hand.

Her eyes widened. "In Surrey?"

Perhaps if she saw his home for herself, if he explained the importance of being accepted into the *Sons of the Conquest*...

But he admitted inwardly he simply wanted to take her there. He squeezed her hand. "Please."

VIRGINIA WATER

ANNE WITHDREW HER hand from Blaise's grasp.

"If things were different," she replied, trying to keep the tremor out of her voice, "I would love to see De Wolfe Hall."

He arched a brow, but she had to continue. Summoning her courage, she looked into the turquoise eyes that drew her despite his outburst the night before. "I'll provide a full report, but I cannot endorse your application."

Passers-by stared and she realized she had shouted to be heard over the din. She moved closer to him and lowered her voice. "Gaetan de Wolfe was a bastard. His father was apparently a Norman, but his mother was a noblewoman by the name of Dacia from Gascony."

When he made no reply, she felt a need to state the obvious. "They weren't married."

He raked a hand through his hair and gaped at her. "Well, *that* I didn't expect."

He walked away, one hand on his hip, the other pressed to his head, then stopped. She couldn't see his face but the set of his shoulders betrayed the disappointment coursing through him.

She hated that she'd hurt him, but at least he hadn't questioned her findings.

Long minutes dragged by. Her knees wobbled, the stress adding to her exhaustion. She was on the point of leaving when he came back. "It's more important now that you come to Virginia Water," he rasped.

She didn't understand and his hooded eyes gave away nothing, but she was too tired to argue further. She was sick of three years of making her own decisions.

Jaw clenched, he took the laptop bag, grabbed her hand and led her to the adjacent Northern Line Tube station. The platform was crowded and they were swept onto the train going south to Waterloo. They had to stand, crushed together with only the safety pole between them. She clung to him, glad of the support of his arm around her waist, the reassuring heat and aroma of his body, despite a determination to feel nothing. If he kissed her now…

The tube train pulled into Waterloo on the south

bank of the Thames. A five minute walk hand-in-hand through crowded tunnels took them to the Southern Rail concourse where Blaise bought her a ticket. He showed his pass at the gate, found her a spot on a bench and wandered off to the end of the platform, mobile in hand, "to get a better signal."

He came back as the train was pulling in. "Just making sure Michael has a room prepared for you," he explained as she got to her feet.

"Michael?"

"Er, he takes care of the house."

"Your housekeeper?"

He made no reply as they boarded and settled into their seats. When he let go of her hand she wanted to wail like a child who suddenly finds herself lost and alone in a department store.

He leaned over. "You look done in. Sleep if you want. I'll wake you when we arrive."

His apparent acceptance of her refusal to endorse his application made her nervous, but a brief nap might renew her energy in case he was plotting his objections for when they arrived.

She closed her eyes. "I'll just grab forty winks."

BLAISE WATCHED ANNE slip into sleep. It was still daylight, but he paid no attention to the scenery flashing by outside the window, his gaze fixed on the steady rise and fall of her breasts. The memory of suckling her hard nipples calmed his fevered brain, though it caused pleasant stirrings at his groin. When she slumped sideways in her seat, he changed his position so her head rested on his arm.

The steward worked his way through the carriage with the refreshment cart, but Blaise waved him past. The fellow nodded and moved on.

He was relieved the setting summer sun had begun to streak the sky with pinks and reds as they neared Virginia Water. Better her first glimpse of De Wolfe Hall be at nighttime, and he'd forewarned Michael to switch the floodlights back on in the grounds. It was a paradox that light disguised the need for a multitude of architectural repairs.

She startled when he shook her awake. She tried to loop the strap of the computer bag over her shoulder, but he took it from her. He stepped down onto the platform first and helped her alight.

His was the only vehicle left in the twenty-four hour car park. He sent a silent prayer of thanks heavenward when his Vauxhall sprang to life and they set off for the home he loved but would soon have to leave.

⋙⋘

GIVEN WHAT LITTLE she knew of Blaise's success at the bar, Anne was surprised he didn't drive a newer luxury car. As if sensing her puzzlement he patted the dashboard once they'd exited the parking lot. "They discontinued this model in 2003. Mine's a 2000, but still going strong."

She got the feeling from the nervousness in his voice there was more to it, but small talk was preferable to silence. "What model is it?"

"Omega," he replied flatly.

"Comfy though," she murmured truthfully. "I don't own a car. It would be a liability in the center of London, but I can see why you need one out here. My bike is more practical."

"It's too far to walk to the house," he agreed, his eyes on the road. "But I've been considering a bike."

A long-buried dream resurfaced. "I've always fancied doing one of those cycling holidays in France," she said, thinking what a wonderful adventure it would be—with Blaise.

He didn't reply and seemed to get more agitated as they drove, leaning forward in his seat, gripping the steering wheel. She searched desperately for something, anything to break the tension. "Is it expensive to park your vehicle all day at the station?"

He glanced sideways at her then switched his attention back to the dark country lane they'd turned on to. "Almost a thousand pounds a year, that's without CCTV."

A double iron gate loomed out of the darkness. Blaise pressed a fob on his keyring and the two sides opened slowly inwards. "Here we are," he rasped. "Home Sweet Home."

She felt like Dorothy coming to the end of the yellow brick road when a very large house with innumerable gables, dormers and tall chimney stacks loomed out of the night. Enormous mullioned Elizabethan windows dominated. A Union Jack fluttered from the flagpole. Lit by floodlights, it looked like a mansion from the set of *Gone with the Wind*—an impressive conglomeration of squares, oblongs and triangles. "It's lovely," she gasped, warmed by a peculiar sense of homecoming. "I didn't expect it to be so big."

WHO KNEW?

MICHAEL GREETED THEM deferentially at the front door. Blaise was relieved to see he'd understood the phone message and was properly dressed. He often traipsed about in his pyjamas and dressing gown later in the evening. "Good evening, sir," he intoned, "and madam."

Anne eyed the butler—no wonder given that he was garbed like a cast member from a Victorian melodrama—but she smiled and returned the greeting, hand extended. "Good evening. You must be Michael. I'm Anne Smith."

His servant looked at her hand as if she'd offered him a poisonous snake. How was she to know the old man prided himself on maintaining what he called "the clear separation of upstairs and downstairs." It was all the more ironic because Michael had been more of a father to him than the inveterate gambler Blaise de Wolfe the Second.

"Cook has prepared a light supper, sir. In the dining room."

Blaise muttered his thanks, clenched his jaw and took Anne by the elbow. She was already glancing round and must have noticed the peeling paint, threadbare rugs and shabby furnishings in the foyer. Once she entered the dining room, the reality he lived with every day would smack her squarely in the face.

Considering she was tired after traveling for hours and had probably worried herself sick over what she had to tell him, she hid her dismay well with a polite smile when he pulled out her chair, lifting it so it wouldn't scrape on the stone floor. His nerves were shot as it was.

He sat across from her and peeled the plastic wrap off the plate of sandwiches on the familiar table, resigned to his fate. There was no point hiding the truth. "As you can see, this is a grand house. It's so old I could show you orifices in the lower floors that used to be latrines. The original manor house was mentioned in the Domesday Book."

He let the impressive part of what he had to tell her sink in, then held his breath. "However, it's a money pit, and to be frank I am drowning in it. Chinese buyers are hammering at the door. I have few options left."

She met his gaze. "I have a strong suspicion this conversation is going to lead to your application to the *Sons of the Conquest*."

"You're a perceptive woman," he replied, praying what he was about to reveal wouldn't alienate her permanently. "I've been assured of a grant of a hundred thousand pounds for renovations."

She shook her head. "Assured?"

"My boss is the President of the SOC."

She snickered. "You work for William Maltravers?"

It wasn't a surprise that Anne knew Maltravers. He'd recommended her after all, but there was an unmistakable edge of disgust in her voice that puzzled him. What other connection could they possibly have? "Yes, he's been after me for years to become a member and when he held out the carrot of the grant…well, it was my last hope to save the house."

Worried by her deep frown, he hurried on. "I also hoped he'd finally make me a full partner once I was a member."

ANNE NIBBLED THE chicken salad sandwich Blaise offered and pondered what her reaction should be to these revelations.

What he couldn't know was that she was co-administrator of the prestigious Montbryce Trust. Very few people knew, but William Maltravers was aware of it because her family's ancestral trust disbursed hundreds of thousands of pounds annually to a whole host of philanthropic and fraternal organisations, including the *Sons of the Conquest*.

She'd challenged Maltravers in the past about the club's male-only policies, threatening to recommend withdrawal of the Trust's support. His recommendation of her services as a genealogist was a thinly-veiled attempt to keep her off his back. He recognized it was only the influence of her older cousin, Irishman Bradick MacLachlainn, that kept her from forcing funds to be withheld until they welcomed women into their ranks. Bradick was a dyed-in-the-wool chauvinist and unfortunately the other co-administrator.

However, if she and Blaise were to marry, she'd become lady of this once-grand jewel. Then she'd have extra ammunition. Bradick would have no choice but to support a family member's application for the grant, or at the very least changes to the rules of membership in the SOC. Loyalty to each other had helped the extensive and powerful Montbryce clan survive and prosper for more than nine hundred years.

She peered into an imaginary crystal ball. If the membership issue came to a court battle, who better to argue it before a judge than Blaise? She understood now why he hadn't been made partner. Maltravers was a throwback to Scrooge himself.

Taking the last bite of the sandwich, she admitted to herself that she had fallen in love with Blaise and wanted to be his wife. However, she didn't want him proposing marriage if he thought it would secure the grant. Now she'd seen the house it was clear why Tessa had left him, and she wanted to strangle the selfish woman. The twit hadn't realized what a treasure she had in Blaise de Wolfe. "I don't know what to say," she lied, dabbing her mouth with the linen napkin.

He pushed the platter to one side, and stretched out his arms to her, both hands palms up. The well-worn table was so wide she could only reach his fingertips.

"You haven't eaten."

Frustration darkened his eyes as he got out of his seat and came around the enormous table to sit next to her. "I'm not hungry for food, Anne," he said, taking hold of her hands. "It's you I want. Please believe I didn't sleep with you because I needed your endorsement. I was smitten when I first saw you looking over the top railing of your house."

The warmth of his hands and the longing in his eyes melted away her doubts, but she couldn't resist teasing. "I think the Savile row suit and the Burberry briefcase did it for me. Not to mention the *old college tie*."

He laughed but then became serious as he stood and lifted the chair out of the way. Her heart did a peculiar flip when he went down on one knee and reached for her hand.

"I can't offer you a grand mansion, Anne. I don't even have a ring to slip on your finger at this very moment, but I'll recover financially once the house is sold. I'm a good barrister, and…"

She had no doubts. "Yes."

He blinked. "But you have to know what you're letting yourself in for. I am after all descended from a bastard."

She leaned forward and kissed his forehead. "But he was a brave and noble bastard and the answer is still yes. I love you, Blaise Emery Quentin de Wolfe."

He cupped her face in his hands. "Don't forget *the Third*."

She loosened his tie. "Will Michael mind if I sleep in your room?"

"Mind?" he said, getting to his feet. "He'll be relieved."

She stood and went into his arms, blatantly pressing the need spiralling between her legs to his hard maleness. "Maybe tonight we could make a start on creating Blaise de Wolfe the Fourth."

He wiggled his eyebrows. "No condom?"

"No condom."

His grin stoked the fire of need building inside her. "I like the sound of that," he rasped.

※※※

TEN MINUTES LATER, Blaise lay naked in his four-poster bed, sifting his fingers through Anne's silky curls while she feasted on his cock.

For the first time in a long while he felt optimistic about the future. The woman he loved didn't care about his financial predicament, and hadn't looked twice at the state of his untidy bedroom. In fact she'd stripped off her clothes and tossed them to the four corners then urged him out of his with the bold assertion she wanted to taste him.

He'd died and gone to heaven.

He had a feeling there was something she wasn't telling him, but his need to be inside her was too great to pause for discussion. He tucked a finger under her chin and tilted her face to look at him. "Ride me," he growled.

She straddled his hips, arched her back and sank onto his arousal, never once taking her smoldering eyes from his. "Anne," he whispered, "I can't tell you how good that feels."

Desire spiralled as she raised up, then sank down again, slowly. "Much better without latex between us," she breathed.

"Faster," he urged, clamping his hands on her hips.

Her eyes lost their focus, the warm sheath heated, her throaty moans of delight grew louder as she rode him, up and down, up and down, hands on her breasts, until she growled out her fulfillment at the very moment his seed filled her. "My thoroughbred," she murmured after collapsing on top of him.

He folded his arms around her, trying to catch his

breath. "Well, that turned out to be not quite true, but as long as you think so."

They lay together in happy silence, breathing together for long minutes until she raised her head to look up at him, her eyes full of love. "The rules of the *Sons of the Conquest* don't take into account that illegitimacy was a fact of life in medieval times. Gaetan's bastardy didn't make him any less important to the Conqueror, who was himself a bastard."

He chuckled. "Ah, the whispered sweet nothings of a lover who's a genealogical researcher," he teased as his sated cock slid from her body.

She feigned a punch to his bicep and rolled onto her side next to him, her arm draped across his chest. "Mock if you will, but even my own ancestor, Ram de Montbryce fathered an illegitimate son, Caedmon FitzRam. You'll meet some of his descendants if my half-cousins come to our wedding."

He put his arm around her shoulders and gathered her closer, his heart full of love and gratitude. "You're a rare find, Anne Smith."

She chuckled. "Soon to be Anne de Wolfe, and just wait till I get my teeth into the SOC."

He wasn't sure what she meant, but none of that

seemed to matter any more. "Speaking of which, how do you feel about getting married here? It's a family tradition. De Wolfe Hall is approved for civil ceremonies."

"Perfect," she cried, climbing back on top of him. "The cousins I told you about will have great ideas about this house."

She kissed him deeply before he had a chance to ask what she was talking about. As their tongues mated he tasted an enticing blend of chicken salad and his own essence. The need to join with her again stirred, banishing every other thought from his brain.

THE PENNY DROPS

After an early morning round of exhilarating sexual delights, in and out of the shower, Anne and Blaise eventually appeared around ten for breakfast.

Michael made no comment, except to wish them *Good Morning* with a slight arch of one brow as he poured their coffee.

She'd soon have to answer the questions Blaise had raised earlier, but there was no harm stringing him along a little while longer. She turned to the butler. "Michael, do you have any experience in the hospitality industry?"

Blaise squeezed her hand when the older man stared at her as if she'd spoken Greek. "Darling, he's spent his whole career ensuring the comfort of our family."

She soldiered on. "So you wouldn't be averse to making sure guests were properly taken care of if we turned this house into, let's say, an exclusive resort."

Both men looked at each other then at her as if she had two heads.

She persevered. "Don't you think this house would make a wonderful hotel?"

More gaping.

Obviously broad hints weren't going to do it. "Let me explain. Members of my extended family found themselves in a similar situation with their properties, many of them far larger and more expensive to keep up than De Wolfe Hall. After the war, one brilliant half-cousin on the FitzRam side proposed they be turned into luxury hotels."

"And where are these properties?" Blaise asked, looking skeptical.

"All over Europe," she replied. "The largest of course is Château Montbryce itself, in Normandy."

Michael gasped. "You belong to the Montbryce family, madam?"

Blaise slapped his palm against his forehead when she nodded. "Good Lord, Anne, it never registered in my feeble brain when you mentioned your ancestors. The Montbryce Trust is one of the most respected philanthropic organisations in the world."

She shrugged. "We have our moments."

"And your funds come from your hotels."

"Among other things."

He scratched his head. "Nobody really knows, I guess."

"Actually, I do," she replied, avoiding her lover's puzzled gaze. "I'm the administrator of the trust. One of them at least."

Michael cleared his throat with a loud *ahem!* "If I might suggest, sir," he interjected, "the nearest Register Office is on Oatlands Drive in Weybridge. You'll need photo identification and thirty-five pounds for the fee. Then you and the surprising Ms. Smith can be married in twenty-eight days."

⟶⟫⟫⟪⟪⟵

IT OCCURRED TO Blaise's confused mind that he ought to stop gaping and say something. Unable to process all the ramifications of Anne's revelations, he decided Michael's suggestion was easier to handle. "And how do you know this?"

"From my laptop, sir."

Now things were really getting weird. "You have a laptop?"

His butler rolled his eyes and turned to Anne. "You'll have to be patient with him, madam, the de Wolfes tend to think we all live in the Dark Ages."

She laughed. "He's had too many shocks in the last few minutes."

"Perhaps. Anyway while you lovebirds hunt up your passports, I'll get the electricity bills."

His butler forestalled the question he was about to ask. "You'll need to prove you reside here. How better to show it than the enormous bills for heat and lights?"

Anne got to her feet. "I'll make sure my passport is in my computer bag."

The fog in Blaise's brain cleared. "Hold on, Anne Smith, if that's your real name, you can't just announce in passing that you control hundreds of thousands of pounds in grants…"

Maybe it was her enigmatic smile, or the word *grants*, but the penny finally dropped. "Oh! The SOC."

She rubbed her hands together gleefully. "Exactly. Maltravers doesn't know what he's in for."

A TOKEN

THEY LAUGHED AND teased like two giddy teenagers on the way back from successfully arranging their wedding details at the Weybridge Register Office the next day. Anne sobered when Blaise pulled into the car park of a Barclay's Bank.

"This is my branch," he explained.

She assumed he planned to get cash out of the machine. "I'll stay here."

Halfway out of the car, Blaise sat back in the driver's seat. "No. I want you to come in."

She smiled smugly, batting her eyelashes. "Can't bear to be away from me for five minutes?"

He wiggled his eyebrows. "Something like that."

They entered the bank hand in hand. To her surprise, Blaise led her to the information counter where he informed the receptionist he had an appointment.

Anne frowned. "I thought you were just getting cash."

He winked. "You thought wrong, Ms. Smith."

The young woman directed them to a side counter where another teller handed Blaise a card. He signed it with a flourish. The teller examined it briefly, then buzzed open a security gate and ushered them through an open safe door into a large windowless vault lined with safety deposit boxes.

"What are we doing here?" Anne murmured as Blaise handed over a key to the bank employee.

"You'll see," he replied with a teasing smile.

The teller turned the key Blaise had given her in one lock of a small box, then used another on a large ring in the other lock. She slid the box from its sleeve. "Do you want to open it here, sir, or in a private room?"

Blaise accepted the thin, flat box. "Definitely in private, please."

She led them to a small cubicle and closed the door as she left. Anne sensed something momentous was about to happen, but what?

Blaise set the box on the counter. "Anne," he began, looking altogether too serious for her liking, "I have been forced to sell off a lot of precious belongings in the last few years, but there has always been one thing I was determined never to part with. I suppose I knew deep-down that one day the right woman would come along."

He smiled finally, levered open the lid and took out a vintage ring box. She had an inkling of what the round leather box contained before he went down on one knee, undid the sweet little hook fastener and opened it.

Blinking away tears, she stared at the exquisite ring nestled in ivory satin—a stunning diamond encircled with sapphires. "I don't know what to say," she whispered.

"This is the only thing of my mother's I have left," he rasped. "I would be honored if you'd accept it as a token of my eternal commitment."

She swallowed the lump in her throat, awed by the love in his turquoise eyes. "The honor will be mine," she replied as he slipped the ring on her finger.

"It's a bit big," he said softly.

"It's perfect," she replied.

A GOLDMINE

BLAISE'S LIFE CHANGED a great deal over the course of the next three weeks. He was blown away by the efficient manner in which Anne contacted all her relatives—and there were seemingly hundreds all over the world—inviting them to the wedding. She explained that it was easy, given that all their names were in the Montbryce Trust database and electronic communications were so much more efficient than old-fashioned methods.

Despite his long and distinguished lineage, Blaise had a difficult time coming up with more than a dozen cousins. It was a painful reminder of how neglect of kinship could scatter a noble line and thus diminish its strength. However, Anne assured him she could probably dig up more branches of his family, given time.

Blaise became acquainted with some of the inner workings of the Montbryce Trust when Anne mentioned the prestigious organisation happened to find itself without a qualified person to head up its legal department.

Maltravers didn't hide his gruff annoyance when Blaise tendered his resignation, and petulantly turned down an invitation to the wedding, citing *conflict of interest* on his part.

Blaise was afraid Anne might laugh herself silly when he passed on that piece of information.

The biggest change, however, was in knowing De Wolfe Hall would be renovated and restored to its former glory. Anne had assured him that even if the SOC grant didn't come through, the project more than met the Trust's criteria for funds.

It was as if digging up his roots had unearthed a goldmine.

※

PLANNING THE WEDDING occupied most of Anne's time, but the researcher in her wouldn't let the matter of Blaise's family rest.

She was determined to reestablish links with members of his extended line that had been lost over generations.

She found an unexpected resource in Michael who provided a great deal of information about Blaise's father. It saddened her to discover that he had been largely responsible for the woeful state of the de Wolfe coffers, and for the alienation of many brothers and cousins. She had names from the research done three generations before, but Michael provided important details that proved invaluable in tracing de Wolfe relatives.

Of greater value was the new appreciation she gained of what Blaise had gone through because of his father's neglect. It was all the more remarkable that he had turned out to be the wonderful man he was.

The certainty that he would make a good father to their children filled her with optimism for the future.

After their first meeting, she'd worried that delving into his history might open Pandora's Box. Instead, she'd ended up finding a treasure of inestimable worth.

GOODBYE

T HE DAY BEFORE the wedding, Blaise backed the Vauxhall in the closest available parking spot near the gates of Margravine Road cemetery.

"I usually come on my bike," Anne said, "but I've probably told you that at least five times in the last half hour since we left Virginia Water."

He engaged the brake, switched off the engine and put a reassuring hand on hers. "You don't have to do this, you know."

She didn't reply, but they both knew a visit to Geoff's grave had to be faced.

"Shall I come with you or do you want me to wait here?"

"It's important you come with me."

He gave no indication of his feelings about her decision as they got out of the car and walked through the gates.

"It's a bit of a hike to the newer part," she told him.

"The cemetery was only reopened in the last few years for burials, having been closed since the 1850's, I believe. I've done lots of grave searches for clients here. Their service is quite efficient."

Blaise took her hand. "It's one of London's Magnificent Seven."

She smiled in surprise. "Yes. The city's seven original cemeteries. Have you been researching?"

He shrugged and tightened his grip on her hand. "Just googling to make sure I had the directions right."

She had dreaded having to say a final goodbye to Geoff, yet as they walked the tree-lined pathways she relaxed. "You should see it in autumn when all these leaves come down."

Blaise too seemed to appreciate the serene beauty of the place. "It's like a park. You'd never imagine we are in the heart of London."

"Yes. It's good they don't allow vehicles."

They carried on in silence for a few minutes. She sensed there was a question in his mind. "You're wondering how often I come here?"

He lifted her hand to his lips as they came to a path lined on both sides by a double row of old graves with blackened headstones, many of them leaning precariously. "I didn't want to ask."

She studied her feet as they walked. "At first I was too angry to come, then I suppose guilt drove me here. Plus, I did miss him."

They paused to admire a huge conifer surrounded by colorful plantings in the center of a roundabout where paths intersected. He put his arms around her waist and pulled her close. "You were lonely. There's no shame in admitting it."

She leaned into him, glad she hadn't come alone. "You're right."

They resumed their walk and eventually came to Geoff's unmistakable grey-white military marker. She let go of Blaise's hand. "For some reason I always feel I should stand to attention," she said with a nervous smile.

He hunkered down to read the epitaph. "Full military funeral, I suppose? Good heavens, I didn't realize he was in the Queen's Lancashire Regiment."

"Yes, and he was horrified by the Daily Mirror's accusations some members of his regiment tortured Iraqis to death. I have come to believe it was one of the reasons he felt the need to go back."

Blaise stood and put an arm around her shoulders.

"Okay?"

Surprised by her own tears, she nodded and swallowed the lump in her throat. She put a hand on top of the slab, relieved to feel the sun's warmth in the rough stone. "I came to say goodbye, Geoff. I'm getting remarried, to a man I love."

The stood together for long minutes, then she linked her arm in Blaise's. "It's over. The anger is gone. Let's go."

※

"I FEEL LIKE a weight has been lifted off me," Anne confessed as they drove south back to De Wolfe Hall.

Blaise kept his eyes on the busy traffic. "Good. We have a bright future ahead of us. No use dragging useless baggage from the past."

It was a forlorn hope that Anne hadn't detected the note of doubt in his voice.

"Did you ever find out what happened to Tessa?" she asked softly.

He pulled over on the Kingston Road, switched off the engine and gripped the steering wheel. "I realize now I didn't love her. I've never given her a thought since meeting you."

Anne reached over and put her hand on his. "Yet in some way she is unfinished business for you, a ghost from the past, just as Geoff was for me. You have to let go of the resentment."

He turned to look into the green eyes he loved. "I'm very glad I came with you to the cemetery, though I admit I had misgivings about it. Geoff was unfinished business for me too."

They leaned towards each other and kissed, then she touched her forehead to his. "It's ludicrous that I never met the woman, yet I want to know what happened to her."

He chuckled. "Hopefully, she's not in some cemetery somewhere. Although…"

Frowning, she took out her mobile. "Let's google her and see. What's her last name?"

"Mulberry."

Her eyes widened as she extracted the stylus. "As in *bush*?"

She hummed the children's rhyme as she typed.

He joined in with the words. "Here we go round the mulberry bush, the mulberry bush, the mulberry bush…"

He managed only the first line before they both

dissolved into a fit of laughter.

Contentment filled his heart. If they unearthed nothing about his ex-fiancée on the internet, Anne had already succeeded in exorcising Tessa from his soul.

A Wedding

"I DOUBT DE Wolfe Hall has ever seen a gathering like this one, sir," Michael whispered. "Certainly not in my time here."

His butler was probably right. The dining room had been cleared and returned to its original purpose as the Great Hall. He wasn't sure where Michael had unearthed all the large floor candelabra that lined the walls and added a warm candlelit glow to the normally cold room.

He had been introduced to so many of Anne's relatives his head was spinning. They'd flown in from various parts of France, England, Germany, Spain, Denmark, even Canada. Every five-star hotel within twenty-five miles of the house was full.

However, he had more pressing things on his mind as he waited anxiously for his bride to arrive in the crowded hall. "True, but do you have the rings?"

Michael produced the gold wedding bands from his

waistcoat pocket. "Of course, and may I say once again what an honor it is to serve as your best man, sir."

He rolled his eyes in feigned annoyance. "I'll give the job to someone else if you don't start calling me Blaise."

"Yes, er, Blaise, sir."

The pleasant background music faded away. The string quartet shuffled their music sheets and began to play the familiar strains of *Greensleeves*. Every smiling face swiveled to the doorway. Blaise flexed his fingers.

As a salute to Gaetan de Wolfe and his Mercian bride, they had decided to wear authentic medieval attire for their wedding. He thought he cut a dashing figure in a black tunic and leggings trimmed with silver brocade, but his mouth fell open and his cock saluted in appreciation when Anne entered, smiling radiantly—at him!

In the ankle-length ivory gown she looked like she'd stepped right out of the eleventh century. The pearl beading, the brocade, the long, long sleeves, the square neckline cut just low enough to display the glorious swell of her breasts, it was all perfect to the last detail. He swallowed the lump in his throat. This vision of perfection was his wife. His Anne.

An Irish cousin, whose name he couldn't at the moment recall, gave her away. He was a pompous chap who'd gone on and on at their first meeting about *selkies*, whatever they were. Some Celtic fairy-tale, he supposed.

Apparently the fellow was the other administrator of the trust, so Blaise shot him a quick smile as he passed Anne's hand into his.

The Registrar from Weybridge had been only too happy to officiate at the social event of the year. The gossip in local pubs had apparently centered on the upcoming nuptials for three weeks.

Someone had mentioned to Blaise there was also a small item about them in *The Times*, but he doubted it.

None of that mattered now as he squeezed Anne's hand. "You are magnificent, my lady."

"You look quite impressive yourself, sir knight."

※※※

As the day of the wedding drew nearer, Anne had feared she might be overly nervous. As soon as she saw Blaise waiting in the hall, a peaceful certainty calmed her heart. She was marrying the right man—this time.

She knew exactly how the Mercian princess felt

when she set eyes on the great warrior Gaetan de Wolfe standing at the door of some medieval church.

Blaise too had fought against almost insurmountable odds to save his family's heritage, and she was happy to have joined the fight—a warrior princess like Ghislaine who came to the aid of Gaetan in his victory at the Battle of Wellesbourne. Her appreciation for Sylvia's translation of the entire document written by Antillius knew no bounds.

De Wolfe Hall had been spruced up for the wedding, and preliminary discussions with the cousins who ran the hospitality side of the Montbryce holdings had been positive. They supported her vision of converting the house to an exclusive resort spa, while keeping one wing for private use.

"Are you ready, Mrs. Smith?" the Registrar asked in hushed tones, jolting her from her daydream.

She took a deep breath, aware this would be the last time anyone would address her by that name, and glad of it. "Yes."

He turned to Blaise. "Are you, Blaise Emery Quentin de Wolfe free lawfully to marry Anne Bryce Smith?"

"I am," he replied.

She could hardly wait to answer in the affirmative when asked the same question.

They each obeyed when the official asked them to repeat the declaration that they were accepting each other as man and wife.

"I understand you've each prepared promises," he said.

Anne held her lover's hands and looked into his mesmerizing eyes. "I, Anne Bryce Smith, give to you, Blaise Emery Quentin de Wolfe, my pledge of loyalty and love. I promise to respect and honor you, sharing your plans and interests, through all the trials and tribulations of life, as well as the joyous times, caring for you in lifelong commitment. I will be your confidante, always ready to share your hopes, dreams and secrets."

His warm hands were moist, tears welled in his beloved eyes. He knew her promises were true.

→》》》《《《←

BLAISE WAS HUMBLED by the love shining in Anne's green eyes. He called upon the warrior spirit of Gaetan de Wolfe to help him be worthy of her trust, took a deep breath and made his promises to the incredible woman whose hand he held and who had brought light to his darkness.

"I, Blaise Emery Quentin de Wolfe, swear to you, Anne Bryce Smith, that I will be your faithful lover, companion and friend, your partner in parenthood, your ally in conflict, your greatest fan.

"I'll be your comrade in adventure, your student and your teacher, your consolation in disappointment, your accomplice in mischief.

"This is my sacred vow to you, my equal in all things."

She squeezed his hand and smiled, letting him know she recognized his deep sincerity.

"The rings, please," the registrar said softly. He held out a silver salver onto which Michael placed the wedding bands Blaise and Anne had chosen the day he'd given her his mother's sapphires.

He could hardly wait for her to see the surprise he'd prepared. He picked up her ring and held it so the candlelight flickered on the inscription engraved on the inside before he slipped it onto her finger. "*Fortis in arduis*," he whispered.

"Strength in times of trouble," she echoed, her chin trembling. "The de Wolfe family motto."

Blaise's thoughtful gesture was all the more meaningful for Anne. It confirmed she'd done the right thing. Smiling, she retrieved Blaise's ring from the salver and couldn't resist a giggle as she showed him the inscription.

He frowned as he read, "*Fide et Virtute*".

"Fidelity and valor," she translated as she slipped the ring on his finger. "The Montbryce credo."

He nodded in understanding.

"I now pronounce you are man and wife," the registrar declared. "You may kiss the bride."

Though the hall was filled with cheering and applauding relatives and well-wishers, for Anne there was only Blaise, the man who had shattered her cocoon of loneliness and despair simply by being who he was. She'd never be able to get enough of the taste of him, the warmth of his lips, the strength of his embrace, the life-giving breath he breathed into her.

HONEYMOON

THE CONCIERGE WHO carried their suitcases into the suite at Château Montbryce refused the generous tip Blaise offered with a Gallic shake of the head and a simple, "*Famille,*" before bowing out of the opulent chamber.

Blaise put his hands on Anne's bottom and drew her to his body. "We won't tell him you're part of the de Wolfe *family* now."

She laughed, content to feel his need pressed against her. "I'm sure he knows we are married. Why else would we be in the honeymoon suite?"

He imitated the concierge's shrug and wiggled his eyebrows. "*Zis ees* France, you know, *madame.*"

She put her arms around his neck and scanned the opulent suite of rooms. "I've been here many times, but never occupied the honeymoon suite."

He frowned. "Not even with Geoff?"

She broke away. "No. His regiment hosted a reunion just after we married so we put off our honeymoon until later."

Blaise sat on the edge of the mattress, testing its firmness. "And later never came."

She sat beside him. "Exactly."

He lay back on the bed and pulled her down. "Wow! Check out the ceiling."

She traced the pattern of the ceiling's gold-leaf filigree in the air. "That's modern of course—part of the refurbishments when it was converted into a hotel. My ancestors would probably have looked up at rafters as they lay in bed."

He must have sensed the pride in her voice. He took her hand and kissed it. "I know how you feel. For all its problems, De Wolfe Hall has always filled me with awe. To know my ancestors slept there since Elizabethan times…well."

She rolled onto her side and twirled a finger in his hair, understanding the emotion that choked off what he wanted to say. However, she couldn't resist teasing. "So you appreciate my pride in ancestors who've lived in this location since before the Conquest. Unlike the de Wolfes, the Montbryces can prove they are descended from Vikings."

He grasped her wrists and pulled her on top of him. "How so?"

She toed off her high heel shoes and lay her head on his chest. "You saw the orchard we drove through when we arrived. Rodrick de Montbryce documented that the seeds and cuttings for the original orchard were brought from Norway by Bryk Kriger, my Viking ancestor. He came with Rollo."

"Impressive," he rasped, kissing the top of her head.

"But that orchard was destroyed by soldiers of Geoffrey of Anjou when Alexandre was *Comte* de Montbryce. They set fire to the trees during the one and only siege the castle ever experienced."

He stroked her hair. "Geoffrey as in the father of King Henry II?"

"Yes. I imagine it was a devastating blow for Alexandre. The estate's apple brandy had been famous for centuries."

Blaise chuckled. "I remember it well from our wedding banquet."

She looked up at him. "You should. You imbibed enough of it!"

He gave her a playful smack on the bottom. "Saucy

wench. Didn't stop me from satisfying my horny wife, though, did it?"

She wriggled against him. "Speaking of which, we should make a start on being the next in a long line of proud Normans to make love in this chamber."

※

THAT WAS ALL the encouragement Blaise needed. He eased Anne off his body. "Remove your clothes, wife, so I can stake my claim to be the first de Wolfe to have sex here. Montbryce's second siege, and you will capitulate."

He sat on the edge of the bed and peeled off his trousers, boxers, shirt and college tie. She removed her skirt and panties, but not the suspender belt and stockings, much to his delight.

He lay back on the bed, growling his euphoria when she straddled him and nestled her warm sheath around his needy cock.

She sank down, taking all of his length, then leaned forward. "You can't prove that," she whispered, her lips tantalizingly close to his.

He'd lost his train of thought. "Prove what?" he rasped.

She rose up and sank down slowly again. "That you're the first de Wolfe to ever sleep here. It's likely Ram de Montbryce and Gaetan de Wolfe knew each other. Maybe Gaetan brought Ghislaine here for their honeymoon."

From somewhere he dredged up the wherewithal to put his hands on her hips and stop her rhythmic movements. "Fascinating as all this talk of the past is…"

She smiled and pressed a fingertip to his lips. "I know. Live for the present."

He grinned. "Exactly. Now take off your top and your bra and let me play with those lovely breasts."

She laughed. "I forgot I had them on."

He chuckled. "They do say history repeats itself."

VICTORY

August 2008

BLAISE SAT IN the comfortable leather armchair in Anne's office on the fourth floor of their Georgian mansion in Pimlico. He bounced fifteen-month-old Gaetan on his knee, chatting away in an effort to distract his red-faced son from the pain of teething.

"And this is the room where Mummy and Daddy first met. She thought I was a pompous ass, which was true."

Gaetan smiled briefly as if he understood, then stuck his fist back in his mouth.

"But soon she fell hopelessly in love with me, and we got married."

"Mamma," Gaetan wailed.

Blaise stood and lifted his son. "I know, I know, it hurts," he soothed, walking back and forth, "but did you know we decided not to name you Blaise de Wolfe the Fourth? We christened you Gaetan after my ancestor who fought at the Battle of Hastings.

"As for your middle name, Bryce, well that's more complicated. You'll understand when you're older."

Chin trembling, the child looked at him, then at the door.

"She'll be home soon," he assured Gaetan, hoping any minute to hear his wife's footsteps in the hall. "She'll be tired. All day in a meeting with William Maltravers and the board of SOC." He tickled his son's tummy. "And she's carrying a baby brother or sister for you in her womb."

"Wooom," Gaetan replied, eyelids drooping.

Blaise chuckled. "A lot is riding on Mummy's meeting, but I don't want to worry you. How about we try beddy bye?"

It would be nothing short of a miracle if the child settled in his cot without his mother kissing him goodnight, but Blaise carried him down to the nursery on the third floor and gave it a try.

His curly-haired son gazed up at the musical mobile that often lulled him to sleep. Blaise hoped the sound of his voice might do the trick. "So you see, if Mummy's meeting didn't go well, the whole issue will go to court, and Daddy will be the barrister arguing the case against Maltravers. Good thing I don't work for him any more, isn't it."

Gaetan laughed, then sat up when the front door slammed. "Mamma."

"Yoo hoo!" Anne called from the front hallway. "I'm home."

Blaise picked up his son and carried him to the landing. He'd expected a shout of victory. "I'll come down."

When he got to the kitchen Anne was sitting at the table, sipping a glass of water. Even in a state of near exhaustion she was beautiful. Gaetan squirmed, reaching for her. She held out her arms to take him and kissed his swollen cheeks. "Poor baby with those teeth."

"Teef," Gaetan agreed, resting his blonde head on her shoulder.

"You look done in, love," Blaise whispered, kissing her softly on the lips.

"I am," she confirmed.

Then she grinned. "But we won!" Her shout of victory startled the baby who stared wide-eyed at his mother, then at his father.

Blaise pounded his fist into his palm. "I knew you would succeed. They didn't have a leg to stand on."

"The board were very cordial and voted unanimously to change the name to *Sons and Daughters of the Conquest*, and to accept women as full members if they qualify."

Blaise raised an eyebrow. "Cordial? Unanimously?"

Gaetan sipped from the glass Anne held to his lips.

"Well, yes, after Maltravers left in a huff. He resigned as president and chairman of the board."

"Ha!"

She lifted Gaetan back to him. "There's more. They offered to fast-track my membership and give me a seat on the board."

"Congratulations! Ironic isn't it? I can't be a member but you will be."

"Not a chance."

He sat next to her, jiggling Gaetan on his lap. "Why not? You must apply. It's your opportunity to make sure they become something more than an old boys' club."

She shrugged. "I can influence that with the Trust. Look what Montbryce money has done for De Wolfe Hall. Magnificent suites, a state-of-the-art gym and spa, long waiting lists."

"You're just going to step away?"

She exhaled, stretching out her enticing long legs.

He put his hand on the baby bump, still awed by the reality he'd created another child with the woman he loved.

She smiled. "I plan to do my research here during the week and vegetate at De Wolfe Hall on the weekends, where I intend to take full advantage of all the spa has to offer. I'm going to be a great mother to Gaetan..." she put her hand atop his... "and the *bun-in-the-oven*, and a wonderful and inventive lover to my amazing husband. How do you like the sound of that, Mr. Blaise de Wolfe the Third?"

"You're already a superlative lover," he replied with a grin, though her promise had stirred a pleasant arousal.

Gaetan rubbed his eyes and yawned, then cupped Blaise's face in his little hands. "Hungree, mummy...daddy."

Anne laughed. "Out of the mouths of babes..."

EPILOGUE

University of Birmingham, Present Day

ANNE FELT PRIVILEGED to be part of a select audience allowed to listen in on Abigail Devlin's defense of the dissertation for her Ph.D. in medieval history. She squirmed in her cushioned seat and leaned her elbows on the too-bright white writing desk that ran the length of the row. "At least the new seats are comfortable," she whispered to Blaise as they watched some of the world's foremost experts in medieval studies assemble at the front of the refurbished lecture theatre. "But why have they lowered the screen? Abigail doesn't have a Powerpoint presentation."

He eased her back and put his arm around her shoulders. "Relax. Everything will go fine."

Inwardly, she knew he was right. She'd spent the better part of a year assisting Abigail with her research into William the Conqueror's *anges de guerre*, thrilled to find a person as immersed in the history of Gaetan de Wolfe as she was. Yet, the winged creatures fluttering in her tummy refused to be still. "But what if they don't accept the authenticity of the *Book of Battle*? I myself was skeptical for a while when Abigail first told me about it."

"That's not going to happen," he reassured her.

Her nervousness increased when she recognized one of the seven members of the adjudicating panel. "Good heavens, they've even seconded Dr. Sorkin from the Sorbonne in Paris. He's the world's leading expert in medieval battles. Abigail's getting nervous. How is she to convince a man who thinks he knows everything there is to know about Hastings that he doesn't?"

"You can only see the back of her head from up here, so how can you know that? Now, stop fussing and enjoy seeing the reactions to the historical bombshell you've helped unleash on the academic world."

She obeyed, gripping the arms of her seat. "Do you think the children are behaving for their nanny?"

When Abigail's advisor came to her feet and cleared her throat, Blaise pressed a finger to his lips. "You worry too much. Gaetan and Ghislaine love Petula."

Strangely, her nerves settled as Dr. Sykes began the

introductions. "We've all had the opportunity to review your dissertation, Abby," she announced. "I believe Dr. Sorkin wishes to begin the inquiry, so let's start."

Time seemed to fly by as Abby explained how she had come across a previously unknown historical document known as the *Book of Battle*, thanks to two men. The emotion in her voice was unmistakable as she introduced Peters Groby and Queensborough Browne, both of whom were seated in the audience. Each lifted a hand to wave at the panel.

Anne swallowed the lump in her own throat and cuddled into Blaise's bicep. They were also aware of what today's events meant to the two men. They were giving a voice to warriors whose names and heroic deeds had been lost to time—the original *band of brothers*.

"Mr. Browne is a direct descendant of Sir Anthony Browne, who was a close confidant of Henry VIII," Abby explained. "Through him I was able to gain access to a medieval journal that had been in the family's possession since the Dissolution. This journal, the *Book of Battle*, was written by a monk, Jathan de Guerre."

Anne leaned close to Blaise's ear. "In a way, Jathan was the first war correspondent," she whispered with a grin. "It's thanks to his description of the Battle of Hastings that we confirmed your ancestor Gaetan was known as *Warwolfe*."

When the balding man in the row in front of them turned round and glared indignantly, her husband squeezed her hand. "I know."

It was true she'd told him the same thing a thousand times, but he never seemed to tire of sharing her delight in the knowledge.

She preened as the renowned experts salivated over the newly-revealed ancient book. Her heart swelled to the point of bursting when Dr. Rapkin mentioned that de Wolfe was still a well-know name, and Abby introduced Blaise as a direct descendent.

She felt the flush rise in her cheeks when Abby publicly acknowledged her help in researching the history of the family and even recommended her company. *Digging Up Your Roots* caused a murmur of amusement to ripple through the audience.

When Abby moved on to discuss the lineages of the other illustrious knights who had come to England so long ago with Gaetan, Blaise took Anne's hand and lifted it to his lips. "I'm so proud of you," he whispered.

"And I am proud to belong to a family with such deep, heroic roots," she replied.

"Like your own Montbryces," he said. "We're the perfect union of two great dynasties."

The man in front turned again, but this time he beamed a big smile.

About Anna

Thank you for reading **_Hungry Like de Wolfe._** If you'd like to leave a review on Amazon, I would appreciate it. Reviews contribute greatly to an author's success.

I'd love you to visit my website and my Facebook page, Anna Markland Novels.

Tweet me @annamarkland, join me on Pinterest, or sign up for my newsletter.

This story is a departure from the medieval world I usually frequent, except of course it has heavy medieval overtones. In most of my books, passion conquers whatever obstacles a hostile medieval world can throw in its path.

Besides writing, I have two addictions-crosswords and genealogy, probably the reason I love research.

I am a fool for cats.

I live on Canada's scenic west coast now, but I was born and raised in the UK and I love breathing life into the history of my homeland.

Escape with me to where romance began.

I hope you come to know and love my cast of characters as much as I do.

I'd like to acknowledge the assistance of my critique partners, Reggi Allder, Jacquie Biggar, Sylvie Grayson and LizAnn Carson.

More Anna Markland

The Montbryce Legacy Anniversary Edition (2018)

I Conquest—Ram & Mabelle, Rhodri & Rhonwen

II Defiance—Hugh & Devona, Antoine & Sybilla

III Redemption—Caedmon & Agneta

IV Vengeance—Ronan & Rhoni

V Birthright—Adam & Rosamunda, Denis & Paulina

The Montbryce Legacy First Edition (2011-2014)

Conquering Passion—Ram & Mabelle, Rhodri & Rhonwen (audiobook available)

If Love Dares Enough—Hugh & Devona, Antoine & Sybilla

Defiant Passion-Rhodri & Rhonwen

A Man of Value—Caedmon & Agneta

Dark Irish Knight—Ronan & Rhoni

Haunted Knights—Adam & Rosamunda, Denis & Paulina

Passion in the Blood—Robert & Dorianne, Baudoin & Carys

Dark and Bright—Rhys & Annalise

The Winds of the Heavens—Rhun & Glain, Rhydderch & Isolda

Dance of Love—Izzy & Farah

Carried Away—Blythe & Dieter

Sweet Taste of Love—Aidan & Nolana

Wild Viking Princess—Ragna & Reider

Hearts and Crowns—Gallien & Peridotte

Fatal Truths—Alex & Elayne

Sinful Passions—Bronson & Grace; Rodrick & Swan

Series featuring the Viking ancestors of my Norman families

The Rover Bold—Bryk & Cathryn

The Rover Defiant—Torstein & Sonja

The Rover Betrayed—Magnus & Judith

Novellas

Maknab's Revenge—Ingram & Ruby

Passion's Fire—Matthew & Brigandine

Banished—Sigmar & Audra

Hungry Like De Wolfe—Blaise & Anne

Unkissable Knight—Dervenn & Victorine

Caledonia Chronicles (Scotland)

Book I Pride of the Clan—Rheade & Margaret

Book II Highland Tides—Braden & Charlotte

Book 2.5 Highland Dawn—Keith & Aurora

Book III Roses Among the Heather—Blair &Susanna, Craig & Timothea

The Von Wolfenberg Dynasty (medieval Europe)

Book 1 Loyal Heart—Sophia & Brandt

Book 2 Courageous Heart—Luther & Francesca

Book 3 Faithful Heart—Kon & Zara

Myth & Mystery

The Taking of Ireland—Sibràn & Aislinn

The Pendray Papers

Highland Betrayal—Morgan & Hannah (audiobook available)

Clash of the Tartans

Kilty Secrets—Ewan & Shona

Kilted at the Altar—Darroch & Isabel

Kilty Pleasures—Broderick & Kyla

Printed in Great Britain
by Amazon